The Magical Espresso Machine

A NOVEL
A Historical Fiction Love Story

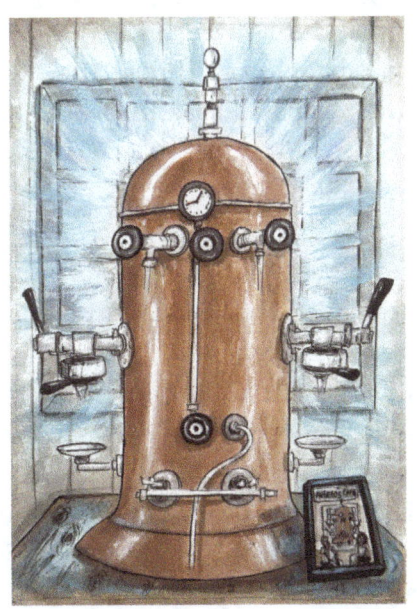

Andrew Louis Botieri

Fine Art Illustrations
by Jesse Morgan IV

Nino-Ida Publishing, Plymouth, Massachusetts

The Magical Espresso Machine
Author: Andrew Louis Botieri

Copyright © 2025 Andrew Louis Botieri
First Edition Hard Cover ISBN 978-0-9853996-3-4
First Edition Paperback ISBN 978-0-9853996-4-1
First Edition Kindle Ebook ISBN 978-0-9853996-5-8

Nino-Ida Publishing
Plymouth, Massachusetts

Cover Design and Fine Art Illustrations by:
Jesse Morgan Design
jmorgan62@gmail.com
jjm4design.com

The names, characters, and events in this work, while inspired by real people and historical incidents, are a fictional product of the author's imagination.

Printed in the United States of America

Contents

Andrew Louis Botieri

Dedication

I dedicate this book to our past, our present, and our future connections. We are all interconnected in some way in our vast universe. There are no coincidences, everything happens for a reason.

For those reading this book who continue to procrastinate about searching for your ancestry in distance lands, I hope my novel inspires you to begin your journey to know your past as it guides you to your future.

Preface

After returning from my fourth trip to Italy visiting family in 2018, I continue to feel so blessed to have this amazing connection with them. My Italian roots from my grandparents on both sides are from Bologna, Cento, Renazzo, and Sant'Agostino in the Emilia Romagna Region of Northern Italy.

During the Covid pandemic in 2020 through 2022, travel to Italy was shutdown.

One day I was contemplating my life and how one decision or event, one way or another could have drastically changed my life's trajectory or even affected if I was born or not.

If I had stayed here on the East Coast and never ventured out West and to the Southwest, how different my life would be. I would never have met the amazing friends or had the incredible business successes I've been blessed to achieve.

With that in mind, during "the lockdown," I, like many people, had a lot of time to think and ponder. My mind took me back to my family in Italy, their stories and how my great-grandparents emigrated to Plymouth, Massachusetts in the 1890s to find a better life for their families. Then I started to think...what if? What if my great-grandparents, Caesar Buttieri and Generosa Trocchi had never met, never married. How would that have changed the trajectory of my life, my family? My grandparents Nino and Ida (Maini)

Botieri, would never have met, and hence, I would never have been born. Weird, hey?

The Magical Espresso Machine is a fictional, historical, love story. It takes us through the early years in Cento and Renazzo in the early 1900s, through World War I, and then we follow the story overseas to the quaint historic fishing village of Plymouth, Massachusetts. This book is also my way of honoring my family in Italy and here in Plymouth. I have changed around some last names, but the characters are my way of honoring their spirit, their influence on my life, and my heritage.

Celebra sempre la tua vita e le tue radici! (Always Celebrate Your Life and Your Roots)

A Brief History of Italy

Italy has never had it easy as a peninsula in Western Europe and the Mediterranean area. For most of its existence it has been under constant turmoil, attacked or ruled by outsiders: 218 BC Hannibal crossed the Pyrenees and invaded Italy, 44 BC the assassination of Julius Caesar, 410 AD the sacking of Rome by the Visigoths, 452 AD Attila the Hun invades Italy, 568 AD the Lombards invade Italy, 1492 AD King Charles VIII of France invades Italy, 1796 AD Napoleon invades Italy, 1805 AD Napoleon crowns himself King of Italy in Milan, 1848 AD First Italian War of Independence, 1859 AD The Second War of Independence, 1861 King Victor Emmanuel II becomes King of Italy, 1866 Third War of Independence.[i]

Prior to 1861, Italy was made up of "little empires," also called fiefdoms or city-states. Most prominent city-states were surrounded by high-walled fortresses to make them self-sufficient and secure from outside forces and attacks. Bologna and Ferrara were the biggest walled city-states in the region of Emilia Romagna. Other city-states around the peninsula included Rome, Florence, San Gimignano, Milan, Genoa, and Naples. Of course, Venice, though not surrounded by stone walls, was surrounded by water. These city-states made their own rules, laws, and were self-governing. They were very independent of each other and self-sufficient. There was no cohesiveness in the country. The rich families of these areas pretty much ruled the countryside. Unification would not be easy as not only politics entered the equation, but many families who were part of the elite had trouble giving up decades of power. Despite considerable industrialization in the past 50 years, Italy remained mostly an agricultural society and over three-quarters of the rural population were landless peasants.[ii]

The country of Italy had just struggled through unification of the many powerful regions and city-states. The Kingdom of Italy existed when Umberto I succeeded his father, King Victor Emmanuel II upon his death. In 1900, Umberto I was assassinated, and his son King Victor Emmanuel III took over the throne.[iii]

During that time, in the rural areas and country-side, however, most families, mainly consisting of farmers, shop owners, regular folk, and peasant day laborers, couldn't be bothered with the new government structure. They didn't trust the elites or the politicians, whether they were liberals, republican, socialists, or radicals; they just focused on what their daily lives consisted of. Doing their daily chores, making their living in the fields or their shops, raising families, bringing their goods and services to market in their local areas and thanking God for all the blessings life gave them.

The government decided, as a country, they could join the rest of the developing world as an important player.[iv] They called the effort *Risorgimento* (Reorganization). The recently unified country of Italy in the early 1900s faced several issues continuously. Italy had a very large debt, very few natural resources, and almost no transportation or industries, except in the north of the country. This combined along with a high ratio of poverty, illiteracy, and an uneven tax structure weighed heavily on the Italian people in the countryside. Regionalism was still strong at the time, and only a small fraction of Italians had voting rights. The Pope was also angry because of losing the city of Rome and the Papal States, and so he initially refused to recognize the Kingdom of Italy. So that's how life was in Italy in the early 1900s.[v]

Another issue challenging Italy was the disorganized education system throughout the country at the time. Italy realized if it was to be a country of strength, power, and influence to join the other world powers, it would need to make a stronger effort to educate its population, not just the elite or politicians. However, the extent of education received also depended on what part of the country you were born in. The north (Rome, Venice, Florence) was much richer and industrialized and the south (Naples, Cambria, Sicily) was much poorer and sort of forgotten about.

If you were rich then your children would have the luxury to go to school, if you lived in rural Italy, either north or south, it was a choice between school or having your children work in the fields or your family business during the day. So, in the north, more specifically the Emilia Romagna region, Cento, Renazzo and the surrounding agricultural areas, families needed their children to help work the big fields, harvest the crops, and help bring the goods to market for the family's survival. Though many had some schooling, it was not their main focus.[vi]

Main Character Family Tree

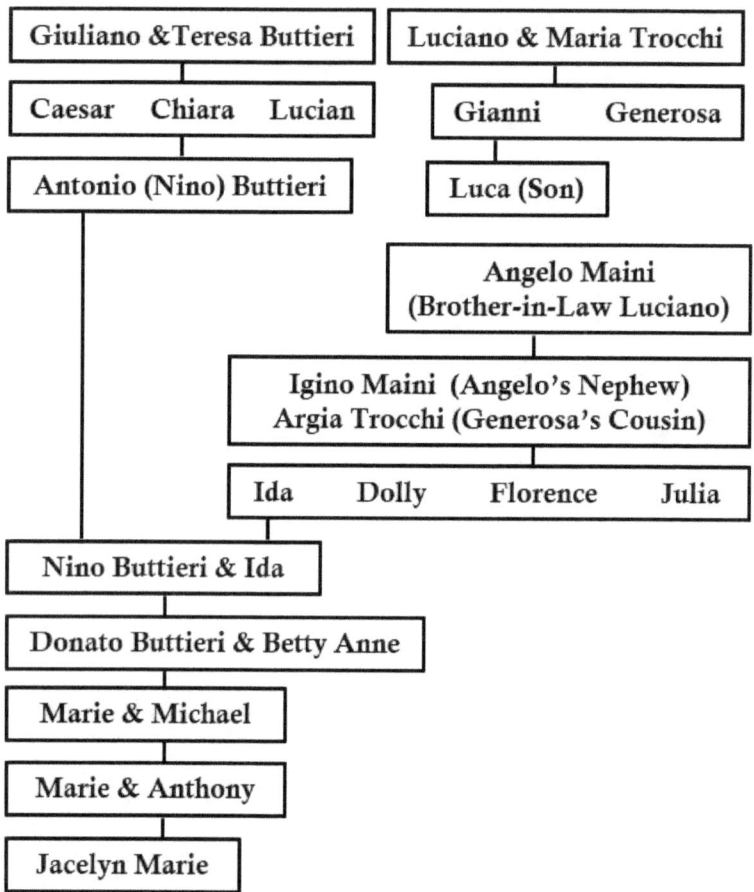

Giuliano & Teresa Buttieri	Luciano & Maria Trocchi
Caesar Chiara Lucian	Gianni Generosa
Antonio (Nino) Buttieri	Luca (Son)

Angelo Maini
(Brother-in-Law Luciano)

Igino Maini (Angelo's Nephew)
Argia Trocchi (Generosa's Cousin)

Ida   Dolly   Florence   Julia

Nino Buttieri & Ida

Donato Buttieri & Betty Anne

Marie & Michael

Marie & Anthony

Jacelyn Marie

Part I

Northern Italy

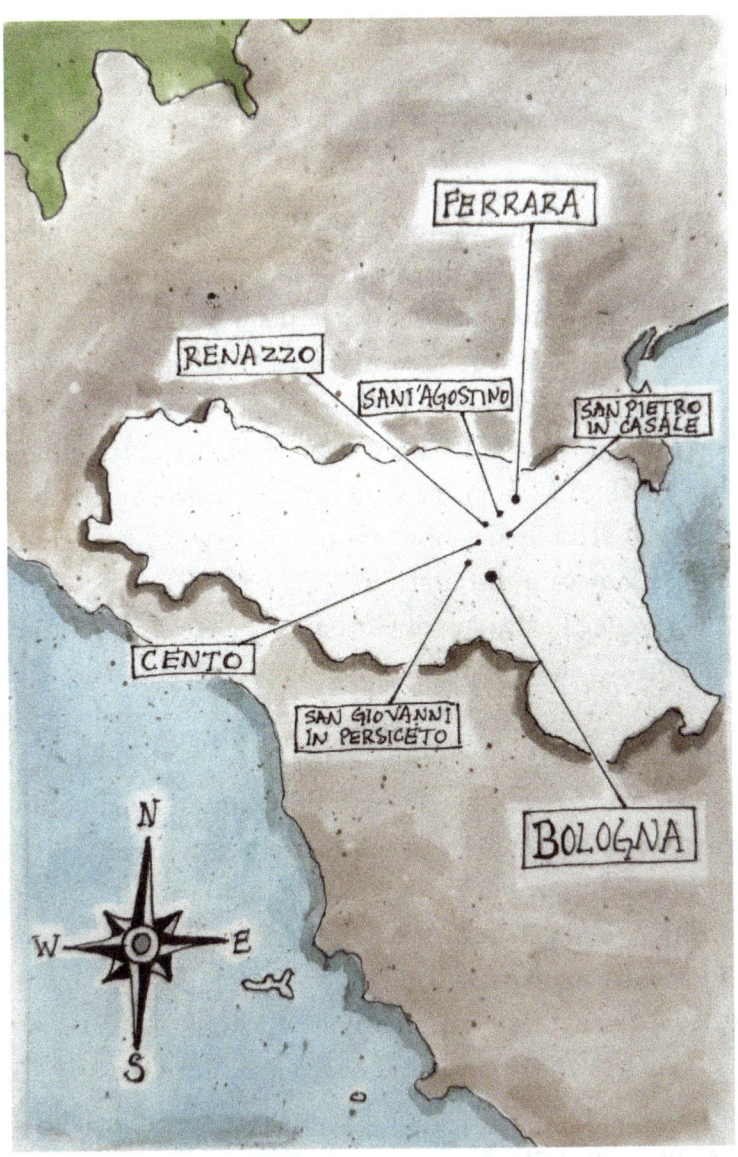

1

Cento-Renazzo–The Early Years (1913)

Cento, Italy

Caesar awoke around 5:30 a.m. as the first clucks and cock-a-doodle-doos from the yard roosters (galli) stirred him from a peaceful sleep. He had gotten used to his daily routine, as he always had to tend to his yard chores first, before he'd go off into his family's large fields and fruit groves to work the land. Land that his family held for generations in the rural town of Cento stretched along the Reno River in the region of San Giovanni in Persiceto.

Caesar is the son of Giuliano and Teresa Buttieri. A rugged, yet shy young man, at fourteen (*quattordici*) years old, Caesar stood about five foot six inches. He was tall for his age, with hazel eyes, medium length black hair, parted down the middle and pushed behind his ears. His complexion was olive, yet he was a little darker due to the long, hot sunny days working in the family's fields. Dimples on both sides of his face emphasized his expressive, infectious smile. You could say, he almost had a permanent, mischievous grin.

A little brown freckle shaped like a cross on his left cheek, lay just below his eye. His mama said it was put there by God to protect him.

He lived with his father, Giuliano; mother, Teresa; and younger brother, Lucian; and sister, Chiara on Via Buttieri, the road named after his family. Living on the same road were Giuliano's brother (*fatello*), Marco, and sister (*sorella*), Poola, and their children, about twelve cousins (*dodici cugini*). Together, Giuliano, his brother, their sister and her husband, Manuelle, and all their kids worked the fields and farms to help grow and gather their crops and take their produce and products to the various open-air markets and grocery stores in the area to sell. They also employed day laborers from the area depending on the season and crop harvesting.

Most markets were within a three- to four-hour ride on horse-drawn wagons. Many times, they would leave early in the morning and not get home until dark. It was a full day; however, their business was very successful.

In all, there were three, two-story family Italian farm homes with whitewashed exteriors, two large barns for tools, equipment, and supplies. Each yard had a large hen house, a corral for the horses and donkeys, and several fenced in pens for the numerous goats, sheep, and pigs.

Outlining the property were large nettle and black locust trees, a four-foot-high wooden fence and a few stone walls with openings to get through to the fields. The black locust trees were ideal, as their clustered white succulent blossoms attracted honeybees for their beehives. The trees grow quickly, and their full leafed limbs would act as a windbreak to keep soil erosion down. They are also sturdy and resist rot, so their large, trimmed limbs were used to build the wooden fences, stalls and corrals on the property.

The roosters were always ready within five to eight minutes of their morning "call to action" after their first alarm. Before jumping out of bed, Caesar would spend a few minutes thinking and daydreaming. He'd clasp his fingers behind his head, still lying on his pillow, and think about what his day was going to be like.

Would the fields be too hot today?...Make sure I bring extra water, as he made a mental note...*If it rains, I'll only have to work in the barn...What was for breakfast?...Would Gino, the local bully, pick a fight with somebody again? What was for lunch? What would be for supper?*

He was always hungry! Though his thoughts often went back to Generosa and the first time they had met. Just thinking of her sent a warm sensation through his body, which made him blush, but it always put a big smile on his face...showing straight white teeth.

+ + +

Caesar first met Generosa when he was twelve and she was eleven. He had finished up his chores that morning and helped bring in the harvest for the day and load the horse drawn wagon. He was getting bored hanging out in the old storage shed, cleaning up all the remnants of the fruits and vegetables from the previous day's harvest.

Usually, it was Giuliano and his brother Marco who went to market, but Marco was helping repair a plowshare harness for the field animals.

"Papa, I have finished my chores, and Uncle Marco is busy with the harness, so can I go with you to the market?" asked Caesar.

"Of course, Caesar. That would be nice, as some-day I hope to turn our family business over to you, your siblings, and your cousins."

Caesar rolled his eyes, as he said, "Si, Papa." Caesar had big dreams, and he knew staying in Cento for his entire life was not one of them. But he didn't say anything to his papa at this point so as not to dis-appoint him.

+++

Cento is located in the province of Ferrara, in the Emilia-Romagna region in northern Italy. Cento is about twenty miles northwest of Bologna and about twenty-five miles southwest of Ferrara, the two larg-est cities for miles. Also, in the municipality, just north of Cento lies the small farming town of Renazzo.

This week's run was to Renazzo to stop at the open-air market and a few stores that sold their cheeses and vegetables. It was a short run, while other towns in the area like Bevilacqua, Pieve di Cento,

Crevalcore, San Giovanni in Persiceto, San Pietro in Casale, Ferrara were a bit farther.

His father, Giuilano, was more than delighted to have his son show interest in the family business. Caesar climbed aboard the wagon, full of long hemp stocks, pears, peaches, lemons, plums, mushrooms, jars of fresh honey, potatoes, zucchini (*zucca*) and an array of tomatoes. Giuliano snapped the reins and the two-horse team of Bella and Bello, bowed their heads, lowered their shoulders and snorted as they dug their muscular hind legs into the dirt and heaved their shoulder harnesses into a slow jolting pull. Within a few seconds, they were out on the main road heading north to Renazzo. Even the horses were glad to get a day off from working in the fields pulling plows and uprooting stumps.

It was a beautiful sunny September day, with only a few whispering clouds above dotting the blue sky. Giuliano made this trip weekly, depending on the crops and the yield from the several fields they had planted that season. The horses, with wagon in tow and its two passengers, left the town limits of Cento and entered Renazzo about an hour later.

As they were approaching the homestead of Luciano Trocchi, his dear old friend from childhood, Giuliano decided to stop in to say hi, since they were ahead of schedule. They had both grown up in Cento. Giuliano hadn't seen his friend Luciano for quite a few months. Yet, the horses seemed to know where they were going. They clickity-clacked over the dirt road and stones into Luciano's yard with their big hooves and came to rest with the wagon under a large shady tree near the front of the house.

Luciano came springing out his front door with a big smile on his face and greeted his old friend with the traditional two kisses on the cheeks.

The two kisses, a traditional greeting among close friends and family, starts with the left cheek first, then the right cheek. It originated during Roman times and demonstrated respect and affection. Luciano grabbed his friend by the shoulders and with a big smile said, "*Buongiorno* (good morning), Giuliano, please come in and join me for an espresso."

"Giorno mio amico," Giuliano responded in turn.

Luciano looked up at Caesar in the wagon and said, "Who's this fine young man? Boy, has he gotten big since last time I saw him."

Giuliano beckoned his son down from the wagon to greet Signore Trocchi. "Don't be shy, Caesar," his father said.

"Wow, what a powerful grip you have young man!" Luciano exclaimed as he and Caesar shook hands.

"*Grazie* (Thank you), Signore Trocchi, buongiorno," Caesar replied.

Giuliano pointed across the yard to the well and said to Caesar, "Take care of the horses while I talk with Luciano. You'll find some buckets over there to water the horses."

After much small talk, Luciano and Giuliano made their way into the house.

Luciano Trocchi was mainly a hemp and wheat farmer. Hemp was the main agricultural plant grown, along with wheat and corn, like many other towns in this region. Hemp was the strongest natural fiber and was used to make rope, clothing, and parchment paper for writing or for wrapping homemade cheeses or cured meats. Being very stringy, hemp was easy to manipulate.

By the late 1890s, hemp farmers and their workers would emigrate to the United States, which opened the door for mass migration of Italians from this area. A prime landing spot for them was Plymouth, Massachusetts where the Plymouth Cordage Company produced rope.

+++

The two men engaged in conversation at the kitchen table about their families, this year's crops, the weather, their dissatisfaction with the local and regional governments.

Once the horses had cooled down, Caesar jumped back up on the wagon and steered them under another shady tree nearer the well. He grabbed two wooden buckets next to the tree, walked over to the well, filled them with cold water, walked back to the wagon, and placed them on the ground in front of the horses. Bella and Bello drank voraciously from the buckets amid snorts and whinnies. Caesar grabbed a couple of apples from the wagon and fed them to the horses.

As he was climbing back on the wagon to wait for his papa, a petite girl about four-feet-eight-inches tall, walked out from behind the barn and strolled over to the wagon.

Looking up at Caesar she said, "Buongiorno."

He noticed how her bright blue eyes glistened in the sun.

"Hi," Caesar said back.

"What is your name?" (*Come ti chiami?*) she asked.

"My name is Caesar and yours?"

"I'm Generosa. What are you doing here?" she inquired, with a bright smile.

Generosa's long, light brown hair was tied behind her head in two ponytails fastened by pink ribbons. Most girls wore their hair up or tied in a scarf for doing their daily chores. Her below-the-calf-length dress that her mother had made was a colorful blue print topped with a white blouse and simple light blue apron.

She was also a spirited young girl, who always spoke her mind, sometimes to her father's displeasure. Generosa's mother, Maria, would always remind her husband that Generosa was just like him. To that comment, Luciano would shake his head and say, "Yes I know, *Mia Bella* (my beautiful), I know."

Shyly Caesar sighed and too quickly averted his eyes, but answered pointing to the back of the wagon with his head, "I am helping my papa take these fruits and vegetables to Renazzo Centrale to sell in the market."

"Do you go to school?" she asked.

Feeling a little self-conscious, not used to such questioning by someone he was just meeting, he answered, "Sometimes, but after I help my papa in the fields and help around the house with my chores. It's almost a full-time job. I do read a lot." Then he added bravely, "Someday I am going to travel the world."

"Do you go to school?" He asked her.

"Yes, I really enjoy reading and math. Though I only go three days a week, the rest of the time I help my mama around the house."

"How old are you?" She asked.

"I'm twelve (*dodici*)!" boasted Caesar proudly.

Without being asked, Generosa said with authority, "I'm ten (*dieci*), but I'll be eleven (*undici*) in six months."

She asked him several more yes-no questions and Caesar sat on the wagon nodding his head, as if he was intently listening to her, but he wasn't.

He started getting annoyed. "Why do you ask so many questions?" he said. Then he mumbled to himself, "*Mi fa male la testa!* " (My head hurts!)

She apologized, "*Mi scusi, per favore,*" (Excuse me, please,) then added, "my mama says I am curious, that's why I ask lots of questions."

Caesar nodded his head as if to suggest her mother was right and said, "Don't you have any chores to do?" hoping she would run off and do them and leave him alone.

"Yes," she said.

"Well, why aren't you doing them?" Caesar retorted.

"I will, but I'm busy talking to you, silly."

Caesar thought to himself, *How lucky am I...ugh...girls!*

+++

After about thirty minutes, Giuliano and Luciano came out of the house and headed toward the wagon as they continued their conversation. As Giuliano got closer to the wagon, he noticed Generosa kept staring at his son. A warm smile spread across his face. He nudged Luciano and nodded toward the two young ones. Luciano just smiled. Luciano's wife, Maria, popped her head out from the kitchen door and said hello to Caesar.

"Giorno Generosa, my goodness you are getting bigger since last time I saw you," said Giuliano.

"Buongiorno, Signore Buttieri, I am almost eleven." Generosa beamed.

Knowing how shy his son was, something he experienced at times himself, as a way to help build Caesar's confidence, Giuliano handed him the reins and said, "You can drive the wagon." Caesar lit up, smiling proudly and grabbed the reins his father offered. With a light snap Bella and Bello sprang into action.

Generosa didn't take her eyes off Caesar. She smiled, sighed, and wished him a fine day, "*Bel giorno. Ciao* (good-bye), Caesar," Generosa shouted and waved as the wagon lurched away.

Giuliano said to Caesar, "So I see you made a new friend?"

"She's a pest," Caesar said, blushing as he looked down at his feet, embarrassed. "And she talks too much!"

Giuliano looked over at him, gave him *the look* and said, "You turn around young man and wave goodbye to that sweet little girl."

Reluctantly, he turned back to look at her, and said "*Ciao*," as he raised his arm in a faint farewell. He realized he hesitated longer than necessary, getting one last look, before turning back to his task at hand.

His papa chuckled, "You sure are a shy boy." Nothing much else was said during their trip to the Renazzo Centrale Market.

When they arrived at the market, Giuliano instructed Caesar to pull the wagon up next to Giordano's General Store. Giordano was one of Giuliano's biggest customers.

Caesar looked over at his father with a look of astonishment on his face and exclaimed, "Wow! Papa, there are a lot of people here."

Giuliano told Caesar that whatever produce was left over, after Giordano bought his share for his store, they would sell the rest to the people at the market.

"Always make sure son, that you double load the wagon so there would be enough to go round.

After about three hours at the market, with most of the fruit, vegetables and honey being purchased by the locals, Giuliano instructed Caesar to consolidate what was left into one of the empty baskets.

On their way home from the market, Giuliano pulled up to a rundown house on the outskirts of Renazzo. He asked Caesar to walk the basket of food up to the front door and knock. A frail elderly man came out, took the basket, patted Caesar on the top of his head and waved to Giuliano. "*Grazie mille* (a thousand thanks), mio amico!" the man yelled. With that he shuffled back into his home and closed the door.

When Caesar climbed back up into the wagon, he looked over at his Papa with an inquisitive look on his face. "Who is that, Papa?"

"That, Caesar, is a dear old friend of mine, Signore Monachelli. He is without means, so I always stop by on my way back from the market if I have extra food to help him out."

Caesar looked over at his Papa with sincere admiration.

"Caesar, we must take care of those who are less fortunate than we are."

Caesar responded, "Papa, if I do this trip by myself someday, I will also stop by Signore Monachelli's and give him some food."

Giuliano looked over at his son with a proud smile.

Along the way home as they passed the turn-off to Generosa's home, Caesar realized he couldn't get that little pest out of his head.

+++

Caesar's morning awakening of daydreaming ended abruptly with another round of farmyard cacophonous galli clucking and crowing. He always thought this second barrage was meant just for him! As his beautiful vision of Generosa faded, he came back to his senses.

"I gotta get up and eat." (*Devo mangia.*)

He sat up, stretched and groaned at the edge of the bed as he looked down and saw his faithful companion, Gatto, lying below him on a handmade hemp rug. Gatto actually means cat, however, when Giuliano first brought the tiny puppy home, Caesar claimed the dog was so small it looked more like a cat. And funny as it was, the name stuck. Caesar had a great sense of humor. Gatto, a *Spinone Italiano* also known as the Italian Pointer[vii], is very sociable with a docile temperament and loves to be around family and activity. His dull white coat with light bronze markings smattered throughout complimenting his lean muscular body.

Gatto looked up at him as if to say, *Let's go buddy...I gotta pee and I'm hungry too.* Caesar wasn't the only one who was ready to eat!

He jumped out of bed, threw on his overalls and dragged himself into the hallway to the family's second floor washroom. He made his way over to the rose colored, ceramic wash bowl *(coppa della lavata)* for his morning "bird bath," which consisted of splashing cold water on his face, neck and occasionally using soap that his mother made in the barn. He combed his wet black hair, tucked the ends behind his ears, swished a mouthful of rose water, before spitting it into a nearby bucket.

Like a person being wooed by the smells from a fresh bakery shop, he headed to the stairs drawn by the aromas of his mother's cucina. As he passed the rooms where his younger sister and brother slept, with a smile on his face, he banged on their doors to wake them up. He always enjoyed this chore. They also had work to do.

Then springing catlike down the stairs, he headed to the kitchen.

Gatto, with his laid-back manner, had already lumbered down the stairs. After Caesar's mama, Teresa, let him out to relieve himself, he was back in the kitchen hovering over his bowl waiting for breakfast, like a hawk circling the blue sky eyeing his next meal. He kept swinging his head back and forth from the "deliverer of his breakfast" to his brown wooden bowl. Caesar handmade the bowl for Gatto when he was a little puppy. He even carved several *G*'s around the rim to decorate it.

+++

Caesar hit the bottom of the stairs and entered the kitchen. He kissed his mama on the cheek and wished her a good morning with several *giornos* and headed for the breakfast table as his mama laid out fresh eggs (*ouovo*), pancetta, fresh panni with buttercream and fresh fruit from their own orchard. Fresh peaches, figs, and sliced tomatoes with olive oil, salt and pepper were his favorites.

But before he could immerse himself in his favorite meal of the day, he bounced over near Gatto, removed a cover from a large wooden bucket and put a heaping scoop of wheat, moistened with leftover chopped meat and vegetable scraps, prepared by his mother the night before. Then Caesar cracked a fresh egg into the mix for extra protein, which gave Gatto extra energy, and helped his skin to be healthy and his coat shiny. Only the best for his dog!

Gatto would wait, hovering and drooling over the bowl...waiting until he heard Caesar's command, "*Manga* (eat)!" which was music to his ears. Then he attacked the bowl like he hadn't eaten in days. Which we know was not the case.

His mother would chuckle and say, "I don't know who eats more, you or your friend over there," pointing her head toward the dog.

Once Gatto was fed, Caesar turned and looked at the breakfast his mother had just laid down on the table for him. He looked like a man on death row awaiting his last meal. He leapt across the kitchen and slid into an open seat at the table. Before he could start, he blessed himself and said his morning prayer of gratitude. Silently he recited his prayer. "Dear Lord, give me your blessings, thank you for this food and watch over my family."

After blessing himself, he dug in, and similar to Gatto, chewing quickly, consumed his breakfast like he hadn't eaten for three days. His mama just looked at him, smiled, shaking her head saying, *"Movala,"* which was an expression that had several meanings...mostly "my little knucklehead." There wasn't much talk at the table in the mornings, as everyone had to eat quickly and run off to do their morning chores, before heading off into the fields for the day. Family conversations happened more at dinnertime, when everyone sat together, eating and sharing stories from their day.

After finishing his second plate of food, his mama inquired with a grin. "Have you had enough?"

He looked up from his plate with a big smile and said, "I'm as full as an egg." (*Sono pieno comè un uovo.*) His mother had heard that expression more than once, and knowing his belly was full always made her happy.

+ + +

Caesar's mother, Teresa, was the kindest and gentlest person he ever knew. However, if you didn't follow her rules, then watch out for the wooden spoon! She was very religious, went to Mass during the week and on Sundays. Teresa was petite, but you could see the strength in her arms, forearms, and shoulders from all the work she did. She had beautiful brown eyes and curly brown hair, wrapped up with a hairnet. She was always smiling, even when Caesar would get into trouble.

Caesar got up from the table and before heading outside to start his day, he leaned over, kissed his mama on the cheek and said, "I love you." (*Ti amo.*)

As he was leaving, his younger siblings were lumbering down the stairs. Chiara was nine (*nove*), and Lucian, seven (*sette*) years old. After breakfast, they would take one of the horses and ride two miles to the little schoolhouse down the road. Their lessons consisted of reading, writing, math, the history of Italy, and a little Latin. Sunday Masses were conducted in Latin. The classes lasted three hours. Once they were over, they would ride back to the farm and run into the house to let Mama know they were home. Of course, this time of year when they were in season, she always gave them a treat of fresh figs. Then, they'd go back outdoors to do their yard chores.

Caesar had little formal schooling, like most children in the Cento area, and for that matter, throughout most agricultural areas of the country. So much of what Caesar learned was on his own. He read books every chance he had. Caesar knew there was a bigger world out there, and he wanted to be a part of it.

Schooling was secondary, as the main industry in the Cento and Renazzo region was agricultural, and children were literally conceived to work in the fields. He still went to school once or twice a week for about two hours. His younger brother and sister went three to four times a week. This was an initiative of Italy realizing if they were to be a strong nation and player on the world stage, they would need to educate their masses. The rest of their schooling took place at home and in the fields.

Before Caesar could get away, Teresa turned and handed him a mug of espresso with a little cream and some biscotti for his papa, who was already hard at work. Before the door slammed behind him, he called for Gatto to follow. Gatto looked up from his empty bowl and scampered out the door. He loved frightening the barn animals by chasing them around the yard. He just wanted them to know who the boss was.

Caesar stepped outside into a warm morning, breeze blowing up from the south. He slapped the side of his leg and Gatto came over, his tongue panting and his tail wagging. The sun had come up over the well-plowed and manicured farmland in the east. From his vantage point, he could see all the fields, the orchards, and the vineyard. He admired all the hard work his papa, aunts, uncles, and cousins put into making their business a success.

He strolled into the barn and filled up a wooden bucket of feed for the chickens (*polli*) and made his way out to the chicken coop. Before he headed out of the barn he went over to his faithful horse, Nico, and brushed him down. Then gave him some fresh water from the rain-filled wooden barrel, some fresh hay, grains and two sliced peaches. Nico would later follow Caesar into the fields so they both could do their day's work.

As Caesar came out of the barn, his papa walked out from around the back side and yelled, "Giorno!"

Caesar wished his papa a good day as well, as he handed him his espresso and biscotti. His papa went over Caesar's field chores for the day, however, he still needed to do his yard chores beforehand. With the help of his cousins, they were to shore up the pig pens, as some of the fencing had come apart letting the pigs roam around the yards and fields, eating the vegetables. After that, they were to start making extra room in the lean-tos for this season's batch of hay they collected and rolled. If they ran out of room, Papa instructed them to build another lean-to. This would take them most of the day. Giuliano leaned in, hugged Caesar and said "OK...off you go!"

Giuliano was a hardworking, God-fearing man, who always put his family first and would do anything to keep them safe and provided for. Giuliano was about five feet seven inches, a stocky guy, though rock solid. He had a great sense of humor and an infectious laugh, like Caesar, but could be stern when needed.

As Caesar made his way to the chicken coop, the rooster swooped in to nip at Caesar's feet pecking for some early breakfast. Just to clear his way, Caesar tossed a handful of seed off to his left, near the rain-water barrel to distract the rooster. Once the rooster was busy, Caesar could enter the chicken coop without confrontation. For added measure Gatto helped by letting out a couple of quick barks warning the rooster to behave. Caesar still carried a scar on his left leg from the overzealous rooster going after the seed from last week. Once fed, Caesar jumped up on Nico and trotted over to his uncle's house to round up some of his cousins.

The feeding of the other animals: four cows, one bull, two oxen, two steers, six calves (*vitelli*), eight goats (*capre*), eight sheep (*pecora*), six horses and a few cats were left to Chiara and Lucian. It was definitely a family affair.

2

The Courtship of Generosa

Over the next few months, Caesar eagerly asked to accompany his papa to the market.

"Oh, now you show interest in our family business or is there another reason?" Giuliano said as he looked over with a grin and a chuckle.

"She's a pest. I told you! Papa, she could talk someone to death."

"Oh and who might you be talking about mio bambino?

"Ah...well...uh... Generosa," said Caesar.

+++

Giuliano found he had a little more time to stop by and see his old friends along the road to the different open markets and store deliveries. Many of them he grew up with in Cento. This time, on their way home after delivering his goods to market in Sant'Agostino, they stopped at Luciano Trocchi's homestead so Giuliano could say hello to his friend.

As they pulled in, Caesar looked around casually for Generosa. As his father stepped down from the wagon, he gave Caesar a special chore. His papa asked him to walk down the road, about a half mile to Signore Gallerani's homestead to pick up some lamb for their dinner tonight. To Caesar's delight, from almost nowhere, Generosa appeared. "Ciao" she said. "What are you doing?" *(Cosa fai?)*

"My papa wants me to go down to Signore Gallerani's to get some lamb for tonight."

Generosa looked up at him and said, "Can I walk with you?"

He was still shy. "I guess," Caesar snorted. So off they went. They talked about each other's day, what their favorite chores were, and the names of their pets. This time the conversation was easy and fun. Caesar didn't feel anxious speaking with her like before. It felt as if he was talking to a close friend. He began to think about her more than he'd like to admit. She obviously already liked being with him.

This time on their way back home, Caesar told his papa of his walk with Generosa. Giuliano, not wanting to pry and make Caesar feel uncomfortable, just smiled and said "Yes, she is a good girl. She comes from good stock."

+ + +

About a month later, Luciano Trocchi had some business to do in Cento Centrale. He loaded up his two-horse wagon along with his kerosine engine he needed to get repaired in Cento. Usually, he fixed all his own farm equipment, but this needed another set of eyes and hands to repair. As he finished tying down the small engine, Generosa came over and asked her papa where he was going.

"Giorno Rosa, I can't seem to get this machine to start, so I need to go to Cento to see my friend Signore Trombino, who can hopefully fix it."

"Can I come with you Papa?" she said hopefully.

"And why would you want to come with me?" her papa said with a grin.

"Well, I would like to go with you to help."

"Any other reason?" her papa said with a wink.

"Well, maybe on our way back we could stop at Signore Buttieri's house so I can say hello to Caesar." She realized she was blushing. "He seems like a nice boy, and I like talking to him."

"OK, but have you finished your house chores yet?"

She quickly answered, "*Si!*" (Yes!)

"OK, go tell your mama you are coming with me, so she doesn't think you ran away," he said with a chuckle.

They both climbed up into the wagon as Luciano snapped the reins as the horses lurched into motion for their short ride to Cento Centrale.

After about fifteen minutes into their ride, Generosa looked over at her papa and asked, "How long will it take for us to get to Signore Buttieri's house?"

"Hold your horses my little one, before we go to Signore Buttieri's, we still need to go into town so I can drop off this engine, and your mama wants me to pick up some supplies. We'll stop on our way home."

"Si, Papa," said Generosa, seemingly a little deflated.

After dropping off the engine at Signore Trombino's home and stopping by the general store, they made their way back home and pulled into the yard of Signore Buttieri.

As they pulled in and hitched their horses to the nearby post, Giuliano came from the house and greeted his friend and Generosa. Just then, Caesar emerged from inside the barn, all dirty from cleaning out the barn and walked over to the wagon, trying to hide his big smile. "Buongiorno, Signore Trocchi. Ciao, Generosa."

"Caesar, while Signore Trocchi and I have an espresso, you get a couple buckets. Fill them with water for their horses."

"Si, Papa."

Generosa went with Caesar over to the well as he filled the buckets. They engaged in some small talk.

Then she said, "Some of my friends are going to meet for Carnivale de Renazzo on Saturday."

This was the biggest festival of the year. At the fair there would be food, live music, arts, parades, crafts, and games for all.

"Are you going?" She asked. "Maybe we can meet with all our friends?"

Caesar couldn't believe Generosa was inviting him to the Carnivale. He said, "I will see if Stefano and a few other friends could also come."

She added with a smile, "My aunt will be there also to keep an eye on us."

He couldn't wait to ask his friends.

+++

The day of the Carnivale arrived, Caesar, Stefano and Andrea were all excited to meet the girls and have fun for the day. They met the girls near the Church of San Sebastiano in Renazzo. When they saw them, the boys got shy and awkward. Caesar quickly walked over to Generosa, and she introduced her friends, Isabella and Katherina and her Aunt Esmeralda, who was their chaperone. Back in those days most times when young men and women got together there would always be a chaperone. Esmeralda was Luciano Trocchi's younger sister, Generosa's aunt (zia).

The first thing they did was find an empty table where they could all sit. The boys sat on one side, while the girls sat on the other. At the end of the table was Esmeralda and her boyfriend Pietro. Generosa made sure she sat across from Caesar.

Sitting at their table, they watched in fascination as the street jugglers, the fire-eaters, and other street performers entertained the crowds. They were all amazed at the colorful costumes and facemasks worn by those marching in the parade as it wound its way around the square. Caesar especially liked the music performers. Generosa looked over at Caesar and kept smiling at him. Even with his shyness, he smiled back.

After the parade passed by, the boys and girls went in search for food. They got an array of local authentic dishes: some roasted lemon chicken, tortellini in broth, crostini bread, and of course some desserts. They brought everything back to the table to share.

It was a full-day and when it was time to leave, everyone said their goodbyes. Generosa went up to Caesar and looked back to see if her aunt was looking, seeing she wasn't, maybe on purpose, she gave Caesar a kiss on the cheek. He blushed so much his face was beet red.

"I hope to see you soon, Caesar!"

++++

Over the next year, life on the farm, and life in Cento went along as usual. Caesar, now sixteen, was still working hard on the farm and still daydreaming of visiting some of the most famous cities he read about in his books and thinking of Generosa.

Though on the horizon there were rumors of a potential conflict between Italy and Austria Hungary.

3

The Sounds of War
Italy and Austria–Hungary (1915)

Since 1882 Italy had formed part of the Triple Alliance along with Germany and their traditional enemy, the Hapsburg Empire of Austria-Hungary, which was still in place when the war started on July 28, 1914. The assassination of Austrian Archduke Franz Ferdinand in Sarajevo lit the fire keg!

In fact, those two countries (Germany and Austria-Hungary) had taken the offensive while the Triple Alliance was supposed to be a defensive alliance against the Triple Entente (France, Britian, and Russia). Moreover, the Triple Alliance recognized that both Italy and Austria-Hungary were interested in the Balkans and required both to consult each other before changing the status quo and to provide compensation for whatever advantage occurred in that area: Austria-Hungary did consult Germany but not Italy before issuing the ultimatum to Serbia and refused any compensation to Italy before the end of the war. So, Italy considered their pact with the Triple Alliance as null and void.[viii]

Italy had vowed never to go to war with Britian, so when the Triple Alliance declared war on the Triple Entente in August of 1914, Italy stayed neutral. Many factions in Italy, wanted the country to align itself with France against Austria-Hungary, since the defeat of Austria-Hungary would mean the liberation of *Italia Irredenta:* those parts of northern Italy that were part of the Austria-Hungary empire. These areas were largely inhabited by Italians, namely Trentino in the north and Littoral (Gorizia, Trieste and neighboring regions) in the northeast. In these regions, support for reunification with Italy was the strongest amongst the middle-class. When war broke out in 1914, many Italians fled from these areas and joined the Italian Army.

A few days after the outbreak of the war, on August 3, 1914, the government, led by the conservative Antonio Salandra, declared that Italy would not commit its troops, maintaining that the Triple Alliance had only a defensive stance and Austria-Hungary had been the aggressor. Thereafter, Salandra and the minister of Foreign Affairs, Sidney Sonnino, began to probe which side would grant the best reward for Italy's entrance into the war or its neutrality.

Although the majority of the cabinet (including former Prime Minister Giovanni Gio) was firmly against intervention, numerous intellectuals, including Socialists such as Ivanoe Bonomi, Leonida Bissolati, and, after October 18, 1914, Benito Mussolini, the future dictator of Italy, declared in favor of intervention, which was then mostly supported by the Nationalist and the Liberal parties. Pro-interventionist socialists believed, once weapons had been distributed to the people, they could have transformed the war into a revolution against the State.

Between August 1914 and May 1915, the Italian Army prepared for the coming conflict. Even before the coming war, Italy had good relations with France, Britian, and Russia. The Austrian government received reports around January 1915 that Italy was preparing to enter the war on the side of the Triple Entente (Britain, France and Russia).

On May 24, 1915, Italy declared war on Austria-Hungary.[ix]

On July 26, 1915, Italy signed the Treaty of London, which promised Italy sweeping territorial gains following an Entente victory. Those territories in northern Italy.

+ + +

Italy began to fight against Austria-Hungary along the northern border, including high up in the now-Italian Alps with very cold winters and along the Isonzo river. The Italian army repeatedly attacked and, despite winning a majority of the battles, suffered heavy losses and made little progress as the mountainous terrain favored the defender.[x]

4
Lightning Strikes–The Photograph (1915)

Caesar and Generosa had now known each other for about four years, since Giuliano Buttieri stopped that day to visit his childhood friend, Luciano Trocchi. Back then, Caesar always thought of her as the little annoying kid who could sometimes be bearable and at other times a pest. But there was something about her he just couldn't get out of his head.

They would see each other whenever Caesar's papa went to market in Renazzo and they stopped by Luciano's or when Luciano would stop by Giuliano's on his way to the Cento Centrale open air market. Caesar and Generosa would always exchange pleasantries, but as time went on, they began to talk more and more. Generosa would make Caesar laugh and would listen intently as Caesar would describe some of the big cities of Europe he learned about from reading his books. She was just enthralled with him. She knew he was the one!

Then one morning, Giuliano instructed Caesar to take the wagon and horses into Cento Centrale to pick up some farm and house supplies. Along the way, Caesar stopped by the home of his good friend, Stefano. Caesar waved to Stefano's mother, who was outside hanging freshly washed laundry on a rope line that stretched between three trees, like a triangle.

With a wave from Caesar, Stefano ran up to the wagon and hopped on up.

"Where are you going, Caesar?"

"I gotta go into town for my papa and get some supplies. Hey and my mama gave me some money for candy and chocolate, wanna come?" he asked while jingling his pocket.

"Si, si!" shouted Stefano.

On their way into town, they talked about playing "calcio"-which means kick (soccer), fishing, the local bully Gino, how hard work was in the fields, and of course girls. Stefano talked about his love interest Sophia. For the first time, Caesar brought up Generosa's name. He didn't say it too loudly, but as he did, he blushed.

When they got into the center of town, Caesar steered the wagon down an alley adjacent to the feed and grain store. They both jumped down from the wagon and Caesar tied up the horses. He made sure they had water and some grain. They walked into the barn area and waved to Giuseppi Zanetti, the owner, who was helping a customer.

"*Un minuto* (One minute), Caesar." Signore Zanetti waved back.

Caesar, with Stefano in tow, walked around the barn to eye the items he needed to pick up. Signore Zanetti walked over and greeted the two boys. After some talk about family, the farming season, and their health, Caesar handed him his list.

"OK, I shall have everything ready for you in thirty minutes, in the meantime go spend your lyre on some candy. I can hear it jingle in your pocket." Giuseppi winked.

They both turned on their heels and ran out of the front of the supply barn as fast as they could. They crossed the street toward Enzo's Market, the keeper of the candy. Enzo's carried many household goods from food to paper products, fruit, vegetables, and especially candy. They hopped up on the raised platform, raced each other past Guido's Barbershop and Vittoria's Café.

Like a hyped-up adolescent teenager, Caesar, in one motion grabbed the door handle, opened the door, and spun himself through the entrance. As he did, someone from inside the store was going from one aisle to another picking out dry goods. In his haste he knocked them to the floor!

Caesar was Mr. Apology! "Scuzi, scuzi, scuzi!" yelled a shrieking Caesar. As Caesar looked down, he realized it was Generosa. "I am so sorry, Generosa— are you hurt?" he said with a hint of fear in his voice.

"I guess I am OK, considering you plowed me over...you knucklehead," she smirked back at him.

"I am so sorry Generosa," Caesar said again pleadingly.

She extended her hand to him and said, "Well, are you going to help me up, Signore Buttieri?"

With his face bright red from embarrassment and shame, Caesar quickly shot his hand to meet hers and briskly lifted her to her feet. Their bodies bumped and as if time had stopped, they stood there staring at each other. Eye to eye. What seemed like a small electrical shock went through Caesar. As he pulled back, out of the corner of his eye, he saw Signora Trocchi slowly making her way up the aisle to where they were standing. The stargazing was over. Caesar snapped out of his "love coma" and quickly said to Signora Trocchi in an awkward way, "How are *you*?"

"Bene, bene, Caesar. How are your mama and papa?"

"They are well, thank you. I'll let them know you asked about them."

"OK then, Rosa, let's go," her mother said, under a mischievous grin as she looked at the two of them. Of course, Caesar blushed.

And then out of the blue, to Caesar's surprise and embarrassment, Generosa inquired to her Mama, "Caesar has asked if I could join him next Saturday for a lemonade at Uncle Angelo's Café? I was thinking I could ask Cousin Julia to join us. Would that be OK?"

Caesar looked on in horror, as his face turned several shades of red. He shot a look over at Stefano for help, but he had his head down with a smirk on his face.

"I think that is a fine idea," said Signora Trocchi, with a smile on her face, knowing her daughter's propensity for boldness.

"Caesar would that be OK with your mama and papa?" she asked. "Caesar?"

Caesar came out of his shock, straightened up his shirt and said, "Si, Signora Trocchi. I will ask them when I get home, but I am sure that will be OK."

And with that, Signora Trocchi and Generosa turned toward the counter to pay for their supplies, in doing so Generosa made a point of placing her hand gently on Caesar's arm, smiled up at him, and walked away. Caesar was dumbfounded! He turned as red as his mama's Bolognese sauce. He didn't say a word.

"Wow...did you see that?" Stefano blurted out.

"See what?" inquired Caesar.

"It felt like a lightning strike. You couldn't feel that Caesar?"

"What? What!" Caesar tried to stammer out.

Stefano chuckled and said with a huge grin on his face, "You two are in love!"

+++

Caesar was sixteen, and Generosa just turned fifteen. He was still trying to find the nerve to ask her father's permission to court her. Even though they weren't officially boyfriend and girlfriend, Generosa seemed to be moving their relationship along quicker than he was. They would see each other around Cento or Renazzo or bump into each other at local festivals.

That night when Caesar got home from his trip to Cento Centrale with Stefano, as they were sitting at the dinner table, Caesar's mother, Teresa, asked, "Why don't you ask to court her? Our family or hers can chaperone."

"Well as a matter of fact, Mama, I saw Generosa and Signora Trocchi at Enzo's today when I was picking up supplies. Well, Generosa and I made plans to meet next week at her Uncle Angelo's Café, if that is OK? Her cousin, Julia will be chaperoning us."

"That is great news," said Teresa, "because she won't hang around too long waiting for you. Someone else will come along and steal her heart. So, I am glad you two are going out."

"So how did this happen?" his curious mama asked.

"Well, well...Generosa brought it up to her mama while we were all talking at Enzo's."

"So, she asked you out?"

"Si, Mama," Caesar responded sheepishly.

Giuliano chuckled and said, "Well I guess it doesn't matter who asked who...it's going to happen and that's a good thing."

Then he added, "As a matter of fact, I saw Signore Trocchi, the other day and said he wondered when you were going to ask his daughter out."

"Papa, he didn't?!" Caesar moaned as he placed his head in his hands out of sheer embarrassment.

+ + +

The big day arrived, and Caesar took the horse-drawn wagon to meet Generosa at her Uncle Angelo's. His papa asked him, since he was going to Renazzo Centrale, if he could drop off some produce at Enzo's Market and then pick up some supplies for his mama. As he pulled up to Angelo's, the weather turned wet and stormy. He met Generosa inside and they sat at the counter on the café stools. Generosa's cousin (*cugina*) Julia sat a couple stools down from them. She was talking to her Uncle Angelo.

After they finished with their small talk, she began to tell Caesar how someday she would like to open a café, just like her uncle Angelo, and sell her baked goods and serve the best espresso and cappuccino in the area. She pointed behind the bar at the espresso machine and said to Caesar, "I want one just like that. I just find they are so magical, because all you need to do is put in the ground espresso beans and water and in minutes you get the best tasting espresso anywhere. That's what I want in my café."

"That's pretty incredible Generosa; I can hear the passion in your voice!"

She was always full of ideas, and he began hanging onto every word, though he would never let on. He wanted so much to tell her how he was feeling, but he started to sweat and get nervous again, so he'd change the conversation to something a little lighter.

She looked at him and said "So Caesar, what about you? What are your dreams?"

Caesar hesitated as he collected his thoughts. "Well as I've mentioned to you before, I love to read and I want to travel to all the countries I've read about, like Germany, Greece, Paris, London, and America."

"Well, what about settling down, having a family?" she asked.

"Oh, there will be time for that later," he said as he looked into her beautiful blue eyes.

Caesar no longer looked at her like he had in past years, as that little pesky girl who always asked too many questions, but now, as a young woman with an engaging smile, full of hopes and dreams, and bolder than most her age. Suddenly, he felt a pang in his heart for the first time. *What was this? What was happening to me?*

She called him out that day sitting in Angelo's. "Caesar, you sometimes look at me as though you have something more to say...and when I think you are going to say it, nothing comes out. We've known each other for many years now, and we are not getting any younger."

Caesar fidgeted and tried making eye contact with her. He did have something to tell her but just couldn't muster up the nerve. As he was about to tell her how he felt, they got interrupted.

Thunder cracked loudly somewhere close by outside. While inside, a photographer friend of Angelo's was taking inside photographs of the café as Angelo wanted to spruce up his walls with some nice pictures.

The photographer walked over to Caesar and Generosa and said, "Look at this young couple...*bella donna* (beautiful lady)! May I take your photograph?" Both Generosa and Caesar blushed with embarrassment but said yes that would be fun.

The photographer made them turn towards him so he could shoot their picture with the counter and café bar in the background. Aside from the two of them, the photographer wanted to show the espresso machine and the Angelo's Café sign in the center top of the picture. As he snapped the picture, a bolt of lightning cracked outside and flooded the inside of the café with an eerie blue light. Everyone jumped! Generosa quickly reached over and tightly grabbed Caesar's arm. It hurt, but he couldn't let her see that. At the same time, he felt a bolt of electricity flow through them.

The photographer was very impressed with how beautiful this young couple looked, so he took several more pictures of them. After finishing, he came over and said he would leave a copy of their photograph in a special envelope with Signore Maini at the end of the week. Caesar and Generosa couldn't believe their luck. They thanked the man at least six times, when another crack of lightning, lit up the sky and café, like a bold exclamation point!

After the photographer walked away, Generosa turned back to Caesar and said with a wry smile, "So you were saying before we were interrupted...?"

Caesar looked at her, stiffened his back and found the confidence to say, "I am going to ask your father if I can court you." He let out a big breath of air.

Generosa chuckled, "What do you think you're doing now?"

"Well, I think it is only appropriate that I ask him officially," Caesar said.

Generosa always liked getting him riled, so with a mischievous smile, she said, "I could ask him."

"Movala, No!" he said, "I can do that," as he wiped the sweat from his forehead.

"OK, so when are you going to ask him?" she said while nudging him with her elbow.

"Well, I plan on riding Nico to your house this week to see your papa, I will ask him then."

"Promise?" Generosa said.

"Yes, I will!"

Generosa leaned in and gave him a long kiss on his cheek. At last, he was on the right track. Caesar felt a rush of warmth enveloping his body, and of course, he blushed!

It seemed the lightning outside the café wasn't the only thing that got struck that day!

+ + +

A few days later Caesar grabbed his horse Nico and rode into Renazzo to Angelo Maini's café to ask if the photographer had dropped off the photograph, he had taken of him and Generosa.

"Ciao, Caesar," Angelo said as reached behind his counter and pulled out a small yellow envelope.

"Grazie mille, Signore Maini," Caesar said excitedly.

"You like a soda pop (*bibita gassata*), Caesar?"

"Si, si, *per favore* (please)," said Caesar. After getting his soda pop, he rushed over to a table, sat down quickly, almost spilling his soda, and anxiously opened the envelope. Inside was the photograph of him and Generosa with the espresso machine in the background.

He blushed when he saw how close he had moved next to her during the picture and felt that pang again in his heart, which made him smile. He grinned as he also noticed their reflection askew on the espresso machine in the background. As he looked at the photo and noticed there was a distorted blue smudge that surrounded the outer edge of the photo. Almost angelic. He could not make sense of it and passed it off as a reflection of a light in the café when the picture was taken.

Signore Maini came over after he saw Caesar open the envelope. "Caesar, Caesar, let me see the beautiful couple."

As Caesar handed the photograph to Angelo, he hesitated and said flatly, "We're just friends."

Signore Maini just chuckled and gave him a wink.

"Signore Maini, do you know why there is a blue light surrounding the photo?"

"Si, the photographer was confused by the blue haze on your photograph, as all the others he took inside my café came out fine. He thinks maybe he overdeveloped it. He also said, 'Maybe it's magic,'" Angelo added with a smile.

After some more small talk about Caesar's parents and the current harvest, Caesar gently placed the photo into the envelope. He couldn't wait to show Generosa.

On his way out the door, Signore Maini said with a big grin, "Caesar, in my opinion you two are more than friends. Ciao!"

That afternoon when Caesar got home, he showed his mama the photograph. He was so excited and animated that Teresa had to laugh. He told her that tomorrow, after his chores, he was going to finally ask Signore Trocchi if he could officially court Generosa.

Even his papa chimed in, "You finally got the nerve to ask him? That's my boy! You are becoming a man," he continued as he patted his son on the back.

Lying in bed that night, all Caesar could think about was Generosa and what their future would look like. Unknown to him, their future was about to change.

5

The War Cometh and Taketh (1916)

It was an overcast, drizzly morning when Caesar awoke at 5:30 am. He washed up, put on his overalls and with Gatto, lumbered down the stairs to join his papa for breakfast before they'd go feed the livestock.

Caesar was excited because today was the day he would ask Signore Trocchi if he could officially court Generosa. He couldn't wait for the day's chores to be done, and then he would dress up and ride his horse, Nico, to Generosa's house to have a "man to man" with Signore Trocchi. Caesar would soon be seventeen.

As he thought about it, his stomach got tied in knots. Would he have the courage to speak to him about his daughter? He sure hoped so.

All of a sudden, a noisy motorized vehicle stopped outside on the road. Within minutes a loud persistent banging thundered from their front door.

"Who could that be at this hour?" said Giuliano. As he opened the door there stood four men dressed in military uniforms. Soldiers.

"What are you doing here?" Giuliano asked. "What is the meaning of this intrusion?"

In the cities of Italy but especially the country-side no one had any faith or trust in their newly formed government. Just look at their dismal track record. The locals only looked out for themselves, their neighbors, and their community.

The sergeant (*sergente*) told Giuliano they have been instructed, by their superiors, to round up all able-bodied young men to fight for the Mother Country against the murderous and thieving Austrians. Giuliano and many of his fellow farmers had heard rumors of the war, but it seemed so far away from their little farm towns.

Like any loving father, Giuliano put his hands up to impede the progress of the soldiers trying to rush into his home. They pushed him aside like a human swatting a fly and knocked him to the floor. While pointing their bolt action rifles at him, Caesar lunged at the soldier who had knocked his father over and was hit squarely on his forehead with the butt of a rifle, knocking him to the floor. He was knocked out cold.

Giuliano's wife, Teresa, came running down the stairs to see her son lying sprawled out on the floor with a gash over his forehead, blood trickling onto the floor. As she ran toward her helpless son, a soldier stood over Caesar, impeding her progress. She kept rushing to get to her injured son, looking at Giuliano and yelling, "Do something!"

But she soon realized a soldier had his rifle pointed at Giuliano saying, "Stop or I will shoot!" *(Fermati o sparer!)*

The soldiers explained they were instructed to round up as many young men sixteen or older to become soldiers, no exceptions. Giuliano pleaded with them that Caesar was only sixteen years old and conscription was for those young men who were eighteen years or older.

Conscription was established in Italy in 1861. Every young man, including disabled, had to serve in the military, in some capacity at the age of eighteen. Compulsory military service.

"That is true," said the sergeant, "but that is for fighting age. These boys, like your son, will be used as resupply teams and to help out at our base camps. In times of war, some laws need to be adjusted. I have my orders."

Giuliano even offered the soldiers cash, but they had their orders. Under his breath, Giuliano cursed his country.

They picked up the dead weight of Caesar and dragged him out the door. Giuliano and Teresa ran after the soldiers as they loaded Caesar onto the transport truck and off they drove down the road. Giuliano could also see several other boys in the back of the transport truck with their heads down as it drove out of sight.

Giuliano and Teresa sank to the ground, holding each other, looking dumbfounded and stunned...as if to say, *What just happened?* It was like a bad dream, a nightmare actually. Caesar's brother and sister came running downstairs and rushed outside asking what all the noise had been. When they heard, both Lucian and Chiara fell to their knees and cried.

Giuliano stormed back into the house and got dressed. "Where are you going?" Teresa asked frantically, still shaking from the morning's trauma.

"I am going to find my son!" Giuliano was ready to chase the truck, but Teresa reminded him that they may hurt Caesar.

"Well, I just can't sit here and do nothing!" he exclaimed.

+ + +

Since the military vehicle headed north, Giuliano decided his first stop was to see his friend Signore Trocchi in Renazzo. He was concerned since Gianni, Luciano's son, was around the same age as Caesar, that maybe the soldiers took him as well.

As Giuliano pulled his horse-drawn wagon into the yard, Luciano stepped outside his front door. He could see the anguish on his friend's face. Giuliano retold the story of what had just happened and how the soldiers just grabbed Caesar, knocked him out, and took off with him.

Giuliano asked, "Have the soldiers been to your house? Is Gianni OK?

46

Luciano said, "They were here, but Gianni was deep in the fields tending to the crops, so when the soldiers only saw me, my wife, and Generosa, they moved on."

"I tried telling the soldiers that conscription was for boys eighteen or older, but they wouldn't listen. This is outrageous!" screamed a red-faced Giuliano. Luciano tried to calm his friend down.

Giuliano was in tears. "What can I do now? My son is gone." Luciano embraced his friend and beckoned him to get into his wagon and Luciano would follow him to the local police (*policia*) back in Cento. The police knew their families very well, and maybe they could tell them what had happened.

When they got to the police station, to Giuliano and Luciano's surprise, Caesar was not the only local boy taken that day. In fact, several boys had been taken that morning. Giuliano knew most of the fathers, but two of the fathers he knew well and their sons, Stefano and Stano. All the fathers at the station were hysterical and in despair.

The police took the information and descriptions from all the families, including photographs, and said they would check with the regional authorities and let them know.

One lieutenant said, "It sounds like a national edict, a conscription, though. Because they are grabbing young men under eighteen years of age, this one seems like a forced conscription."

Another officer added, "Rumor is they are losing a lot of young fighting men at the front against Austria and need to replenish their forces." The police said they didn't have much power to do anything, but they would let the families know what they could find out.

Giuliano and other families were distraught. They looked like zombies coming out of the police station. Luciano guided his old friend back to his wagon and followed him to his house. Teresa came running out before the horses even made it into the yard, along with Gatto.

"Did you get any news?" she screamed hysterically.

Giuliano, whose head was slumped down into his chest, looked up with tears in his eyes. He slowly shook his head and said, "No."

As he got down from his wagon, Teresa came running over and hugged her husband, with Gatto jumping around anxiously. They both fell down in tears.

Giuliano looked at his friend Luciano and said through a cracked and broken voice, "Grazie mille amico." Luciano stayed in his wagon until Giuliano and his wife slowly walked back into their home.

When Luciano arrived back home, Generosa was standing by the door with a look of dismay and bewilderment on her face. Her mother had told her the little that she knew about the morning's event and that Caesar was taken away by soldiers.

She ran up to her papa and frantically tugged on his coat. "What happened Papa? Where is Caesar?"

With tears in his eyes, he said, "We don't know yet my angel...we just don't know." At that, Generosa burst into tears and ran into her house.

6

The Convoy Heads North

The army transport truck headed northeast toward Ferrara for the one-hour truck ride, where the group would be transferred to waiting trains and then journey northward to Padua and then onto Portogruaro to their base camp. Portogruaro was closer to the frontlines. The transport trucks kept stopping along the way to pick up new "recruits."

Caesar was still in a daze, still in shock at what had just happened. He still had blood trickling down his forehead across his cheeks and a lump growing on his head. *How could his government do this to him and these other boys?* he thought. As more farm boys were loaded onto the truck, Caesar overheard one of the soldiers in the front seat saying that the government was low on fighters and needed to collect as many young men as possible. From what Caesar could also hear, the transport vehicles were heading to Ferrara to the trains. As of this date, Austria controlled a large chunk of northern Italy that the Italian government was hoping to take back during this conflict.

By now Caesar was getting his wits back from the rifle butt to the head. He looked up and down the bench he was sitting on and looked across to the other side, from one end to the other...filled with boys around his age, all looking bewildered and frightened.

In fact, he recognized a couple of them. One was Stefano, just across from him, a friend who had accompanied him to the Festival with Generosa. Stefano also played soccer with Caesar, in the Cento league. His father and Papa were friendly with each other. Stefano was about the same size as Caesar, but more muscular. His hair was shorter but also parted down the middle and his eyes were deep blue.

Caesar whispered over, "Hey, Stefano, I see they took you too."

Stefano raised his head dejectedly and looked at Caesar with fear and tears in his eyes. Stefano told a similar story of how he was on his way to his father's field when a motorized vehicle of soldiers stopped him on the side of the road. They asked him a few questions and then *strongly* urged him to get into the truck. At first Stefano said, "No."

Then a soldier holding a rifle said, "If you don't, we have orders to shoot you as a traitor."

Caesar shook his head sadly and said to Stefano, "We will have to look after each other."

Stefano started to whimper and said, "I don't think my parents even know what happened to me."

Before he could respond, Caesar was distracted by a boy who was crying on the bench across from him near Stefano. The boy's head was down, and his shoulders were heaving as he sobbed. Something about the boy looked familiar to Caesar, but he couldn't quite place him.

After a while, the boy looked up with red, swollen eyes. It was Gino, the bully from Cento. He looked over at Caesar and acknowledged him with a nod. Gino was a year older than Caesar, a few inches shorter and a little chubby, which made him a good bully. His brown hair was cropped close to his head and matched his brown eyes.

Then Caesar asked, "What happened, Gino?"

Through a crackling voice Gino said he had finished eating breakfast with his mama and had just gone outside to feed the animals, when all of a sudden, two transport trucks with large benches in the back, covered with a tarp, pulled up and began talking to him about "loyalty to country" and "We need young courageous men to help fight our enemies."

Gino said his mama came rushing out trying to explain to the officer in charge that her son was only seventeen, her only child, and she was a widow who needed him in the fields to help support and feed her family.

Still, at gun point, Gino was roughly escorted over to the truck. His mother started to scream, crying, and began hitting one of the soldiers on his back with her fists.

Gino sobbed, "They told her if she continued, they would shoot her. I was given no more than a few seconds to go over, give her a hug and a kiss on the forehead. I told her it would be OK, that I'd be back soon."

"That's almost exactly how it happened to me," Caesar said.

Then Gino looked at Caesar and said, "What do we do now, Caesar?"

How ironic Caesar thought. Here is this bully who used to intimidate everyone, punch and push those who were smaller, weaker than him, and now he's asking me, *What are we going to do?*

At first, Caesar was going to say something unkind, but he knew that wasn't the right thing to do. So, he said, "Gino, you, me, and Stefano need to stick together, OK? We'll find a way out of this." After those words came out of his mouth, all Caesar could think was, *There's no way we're returning home without fighting.*

+++

Late in the afternoon, the transport vehicles pulled off the road and into a field near the train station at Ferrara. They were all led out of the back of the truck, given a blanket, bread, fruit, and water, and told to bed down inside the train cars for the night. They were all warned there would be guards posted, so no one was to be foolish and try to run away...or they would be shot.

The next morning, after a sleep full of anxiety and uncertainty and a quick breakfast, they were all herded back onto the trains for the long three-hour-plus ride to Portogruaro. The train would make various stops on the way, picking up other young men to fight for the Mother Country.

7

The Search for Caesar Continues

A few days later, Giuliano, once again, stopped by the police station on his way back from the market to see if there was any word about Caesar and the other boys. All he had to do was walk into the station and see the empty look on the faces of the policia, and he knew there was no information.

One officer came up to Giuliano and told him other municipalities nearby had reported the same experience. It appears a rogue sergeant was looking to make a name for himself by skirting the conscription age and taking men younger than eighteen. "I guess he was looking to fill some quota on recruiting young men to fight."

"This is an outrage! My son is only sixteen!" yelled Giuliano.

The police officer, who he knew, tried to calm Giuliano down and assured him they would continue to investigate. Giuliano left dejected.

The following day Signore Trocchi with Generosa and Gianni tagging along, pulled his horse-drawn wagon into the Buttieri homestead. Giuliano and his other son, Lucian, were just coming in from the fields. Signore Trocchi gave his old friend a wave. "Any news on Caesar?" he said.

As Giuliano looked up at his friend with hunched shoulders, tears began to well up in his eyes and cascade down his cheeks. "The Lieutenant came by yesterday and said they have tried everything they could possibly do, and they are getting no answers from anyone. I guess my son is gone."

Giuliano looked over at Generosa and said, "I am sorry young lady."

She began to cry uncontrollably. Gianni pulled her to his shoulder as she continued to sob.

"Mille grazie Luciano for coming by," said Giuliano. "I must get back to work, it helps me get through the day."

Signore Trocchi hung his head as a few tears rolled down his cheeks, thinking how close he came to losing Gianni. He felt heartsick for his long-time friend.

"We will continue to pray for Caesar's safe return. Ciao mio amico." He snapped the reins, and his wagon lurched into motion for the ride back to Renazzo. Giuliano just stood there, waved goodbye, then slowly turned back to the barn to finish his chores.

Since the day Caesar was taken, Gatto would lie by the edge of the road in front of the house. Giuliano would have to beckon him in at night. Gatto would reluctantly stagger into the house with a sad look on his face. In the mornings, he would be at the front door, whining, waiting to be let out, where he would continue to lie at the edge of the road, waiting for Caesar.

8

Arriving at the Frontlines (Monfalcone)

The train pulled into the Portogruaro station where they were met by several transport vehicles. The recruits were loaded into the vehicles and wagons and headed northeast toward the base camp, which was about three plus hours by caravan west of Monfalcone, one of the many fronts of the war. Monfalcone means "Falcon Mountain." They were near the Italian/Austrian frontlines.

The trucks and wagons pulled right into a well-organized military camp and headquarters in a large open area about the size of eight football fields. All tents were camouflaged to blend in with their surroundings. It was late afternoon. The sun was beginning to set over the treetops.

When the trucks stopped, a brutish looking soldier, with a thick body, a mean demeanor, and an Italian hooked nose carrying a Vetterli M1887 bolt-action repeating rifle, met the convoy. He threw open the brown canvas covering the back of the truck.

He notified each recruit as they got off the truck, "We're now near the frontline of the war. If anyone has any idea of running away, you will be shot dead in your tracks and your families would also be harmed. "*Capito* (Understand)?" said the soldier.

Almost everyone nodded in unison as their heads bobbed yes. They all looked disheveled with looks of confusion and bewilderment emanating from their disheartened faces. In the background, they could hear the sounds of war far in the distance, bombs exploding and the roar of planes in the air. The look of shock on their faces was widespread.

At that moment another soldier came up to the soldier shouting orders at the recruits and said, "Benito, I am here to relieve you."

Benito said in return, "Keep an eye on them and if they step out of line, punish them." The soldier was Benito Mussolini, who had been drafted into the army in mid-1915, though he was initially opposed to the war with Austria/Hungary. He would be promoted quickly through the ranks due to his known, vicious and aggressive demeanor. He was born under the sign of Leo. Benito Mussolini, along with some of the other troops were part of the famed Bersaglieri unit.

As the line of new soldiers shuffled along, in the distance, they could hear the sounds of exploding ordnances. They were still trying to figure out what the hell happened to them and what they do now. Two of the young recruits in the front of the line started yelling and shoving the sergeant and screaming, "You have no right to take us from our homes without our parent's approval! We are too young to serve in the army! Let us go now!"

The sergeant didn't even hesitate...he pulled out his Italian-made Bodeo 1889 revolver, a six shooter. Its white metal body glimmering off the setting sunlight. He put the gun up to the head of the complaining recruit and pulled the trigger. The young man dropped lifelessly dead to the ground, blood and brains spewing all over, even spraying the recruits nearby. The blood then being absorbed into the earth as quickly as it was flowing out of his head wound.

The cracking sound from the gun shocked and jolted everyone; some ducked, some tried to hide, others just fell to the ground. But the message was clearly sent. *If you try to run away or try to rebel against us, you will be shot.*

Caesar looked over at his friends and whispered, "Now I am scared." Instead of dragging the body away, they left it there for a couple days as a stark reminder.

Looking around, they saw over one hundred, four- to eight-man pitched green canvas tents, stretching out across the southwest corner of the large field. Six extra-large canvas tents, each about half the size of a football field, were located on the southeast side. These were the headquarters for the top military brass, lieutenants, sergeants, other military officials, and the war room. This would be their base of operations for their resupply missions to the troops at the Monfalcone front.

The mess halls were two large tents, about 200 feet in length and 75 feet across. Even with their large size, mealtimes still had to be staggered to accommodate their numbers. Conveniently, the officer's tents were within a short walk to their next meal or pot of coffee.

The field hospitals took up the most space. Unlike the mess hall, soldiers' quarters, and the quarters of the "important" personnel, the field hospital tents were placed about 75 yards away from everything to limit the gruesome site of watching the wounded going in and out of the tents for treatment, coming out on a stretcher with a white sheet covering the dead, and of course, diminishing the loud screams of the wounded as they were being operated on.

In between the field hospital and the rest of the personnel, the army parked its heavy equipment, tanks, supply trucks, military hardware, the transport vehicles, and the wagons, to help reduce the sounds of death and injury reaching the soldiers' ears.

All in all, there were about 1200 personnel in the camp. About once a week about 200 to 300 soldiers/workers would rotate from the base camp to the front. The returning soldiers would get required medical attention, rest and replenishment before going back to the front.

Even though it was such a traumatic day for Caesar and his fellow recruits, his stomach began to growl when he saw the mess tents. They weren't hard to locate, since it was lunchtime, he saw dozens of men coming out with tin food plates stacked with meat sandwiches, ricotta cakes, fruit, and tin cups of coffee. *I'm starving!* he thought to himself.

Caesar reminded Stefano and Gino they should stick together, so they all got in line behind each other. They were then given a piece of paper with a number on it and were shoved along toward the supply tent in front of them, next to the mess tent. The new soldiers, about seventy-five of them, entered where above them a sign read, "Fight For Your Mother Country" (*Combatti per la Tua Madrepatria*).

They were directed to go over to a row of six-foot-long tables to check in, give their name, and hand over the piece of paper they were given. They then receive their military uniform, which included a pair of boots, socks, and a backpack of personal supplies including chocolate bars, a small first aid kit, soap, a towel, some candles, matches, a shaving kit, and a tin cup for water, coffee, or soup.

Once they received these items they went directly to their four-man tent. Luckily, Caesar, Stefano, and Gino got to be in the same tent, along with another recruit named Stano, who was also from the Cento area. Stano came from Casoni, just south of Cento, but knew of Caesar's family farming operation.

They changed into their fatigues and were instructed to place their old clothes outside of the tent. Later someone came by to collect them. The idea was if the young soldiers escaped it would be easier to find them in their military fatigues than in street clothes. They were told to keep their shoes; in case they wore holes in their boots. On the ground in front of each of them was a thin blanket to lie on as a cushion and two thicker blankets. One thick blanket was to place over your body, the other was to roll up to place under your head. They all kept an extra shirt and rolled it up in their blanket for a thicker pillow. After settling in, they all blew out a sigh of relief, looked at each other, still wondering if what was happening was real or a dream. Once again Caesar said to the boys, "Don't forget, we must stick together. No matter what!"

A loud voice startled them from outside shouting, *"Assemblare! Assemblare!"* (Assemble! Assemble!) The four rushed out of their tent, stood upright, straightening out their new uniforms and looked across at all the other young men standing outside of their tents as well. The sun continued to fall, and it was getting darker.

They were led into one of the mess tents and stood in line. As they moved along, many of the food items plopped on their plates were indistinguishable. Caesar looked up at the server each time the spoon hit his plate, looked at the clump of food, then looked back at the server, as if to say, "What is this?"

The server, with a smirk on his face said, "It's better than your mama's cooking." Caesar looked at him with a scowl, grabbed two pieces of bread and went to find a place to sit down. He wondered if Gatto would even eat this slop.

They sat together in the corner. Gino wasn't saying much, though both he, Stano, and Stefano looked to Caesar for guidance. Even though Caesar was always hungry, he was also a picky eater. He pushed his spoon through the "mud" *(fango)*, as he called it, and put it to his nose. It smelled like a mixture of stale pasta and vermicelli, mixed with an acidic red sauce.

Where was the fresh cheese, he thought. He looked around and realized there were only large chunks of parmesan cheese on a side table, but nothing was grated like his mother did. He sadly smirked to himself.

After chow, a lieutenant named Scribini, spewed out a government inspired propaganda rant: "It is important to fight for your Mother Country and win back vital territory the Austrians stole from us! It is time to step up and protect the survival of Italy! Even if you have to give your life for your country!"

These "stolen lands" are called irredente lands where the majority of that region's people speak their Italian language and practice their culture, and they want those lands back. After the Capture of Rome in 1870, almost the whole of Italy was united in a single state, the Kingdom of Italy. Among the irredente lands still belonging to Austria-Hungary were the city of Fiume, Trentino-Alto Adige, and Dalmatia in the northern part of the country.

At the end of dinner, Mussolini jumped to his feet and screamed, *"Viva Italia! Viva Italia!"* (Long live Italy! Long live Italy!) shoving his arm and open hand salute into the air and encouraged everyone else to do the same.

Everyone near him was so scared not to follow his direction, for fear of being punished or killed, they all in awkward unison, threw their hands into the air.

"Viva Italia! Viva Italia!" the crowd was screaming, crazed. As Caesar looked around the room, he saw not everyone was so enthusiastic. The Mussolini style salute would eventually be replicated by Adolf Hitler.

After the talk, they were instructed to go to their tents and get a good night's sleep, for tomorrow they would begin calisthenics and military drills. As the boys bedded down for the night, there was little conversation. Stano lit a candle so they could at least see inside the tent as they laid out their beds and talked for a while. They were still in a state of disbelief. Stefano was the first to speak, "Did you see all those boys saluting and cheering? It was scary!"

"It truly was," said Caesar. "I wonder how many realize that some of us may die during this war, a war we didn't ask to be involved in?"

Gino spoke up, "I wonder if our families are looking for us?"

"Knowing my papa and Caesar's papa I am sure they are," said Stefano. "I still don't know if my family even knows what happened to me." Then he added, "One minute I was in the fields, the next minute I am on a vehicle being kidnapped."

After a prayer, Stano blew out the candle.

That night Caesar thought of Generosa and his family. What they must be going through. He longed for Generosa. He couldn't imagine his bad luck, abducted on the day he was going to ask her papa if he could court her. Or was it the other day? He had lost complete sense of time. He and his compadres were scared, but also exhausted, and finally fell asleep to the occasional sounds of explosions in the background.

9

First Day of Military Camp Life (1916)

The next morning around 5:00 a.m., they were awoken by the sound of an off-tune bugle, making so much noise most boys shot out of bed like a cannon ball. It reminded Caesar of the noises his burro, Petra, made back at the family farm. They got up, dressed in their new fatigues, splashed water on their faces, ready to go to the mess tent to eat breakfast.

As soon as Caesar opened the tent flap to step outside, he could smell the aroma coming from the mess tent. His stomach growled to the point that Stefano looked over at him and said, "I can hear your hungry belly from here." They both chuckled.

Breakfast (*colazione*) consisted of lots of bread (*pane*), cheeses, eggs, meats, espresso coffee, water, and fresh fruit...if you wanted to call, over ripened fruit, fresh. Even though Caesar was very picky about his food, this was about feeding his growling monster, plain and simple. He even stuffed some extra bread into his pockets for later.

After shoveling their food down, they were hurried into formation in between their tents and where the military equipment was staged to begin their drills. They lined up into rows of ten and about ten deep. Their instructor ran them through some stretching exercises, then jumping jacks, push-ups, sit-ups, and a few other exercises. After a ten-minute rest, they were led by another instructor who had them run three laps around the perimeter of the camp. When they got back to the exercise area many boys fell to the ground in complete exhaustion. Other boys, who worked all day in the fields and were in better shape, just leaned over grabbing their knees to catch their breath. Of course, Caesar and Stefano were in this group.

After a quick lunch (*pranzo*), consisting of sandwiches of salami, mortadella, provolone and water, the boys were instructed how to load up the two horse-drawn wagons and motorized vehicles with supplies, weapons, and ammo for the three-hour ride to Monfalcone on the front. They loaded boxes of dynamite, bullets, Vetterli bolt action rifles, bayonets, boxes of food, breads, fruits, eggs, bacon tins, and large containers of water. They needed to be loaded properly to keep the weapons from being tipped over on the rough terrain or damaged as well as the eggs from breaking. All-important supplies! There were also a few boxes marked "Top Military Only." Caesar figured out these were bottles of fine wine, port, high quality cigars, and cigarettes.

This routine continued for the first month, then their training began to take on a different shape. It now consisted of marching in order with their empty Vetterli rifles over their shoulders, carrying heavy boxes around the camp to strengthen their legs and upper body, practicing the use of their bayonets on cloth stuffed dummies and shooting at straw targets about fifty yards away. The targets were made to look like men in Austrian uniforms. *I guess visualization was what they wanted,* Caesar thought.

They were only allowed six bullets per round. Several privates would run up and down the rifle line, handing them additional ammunition. Around 10:00 a.m. they took a water break as Caesar, Stefano, Stano, and Gino stood in a circle with some other boys from their group, each keeping their eyes up and voices down as they tried cheering each other up. Caesar seemed to be the born leader of this small group of about eight boys.

They went back to drills and then more target and bayonet practice. Then, early afternoon, Benito Mussolini told the group that they would be going on their first resupply mission early next week to the frontlines. Caesar, Stefano, and Stano tried to stay stoic, while Gino bent over and grabbed himself by the knees, and his eyes began to well up. The others just looked at each other in horror.

"I know things look bleak guys, but we need to be strong and help support each other; it won't be easy, but we are strong...viva Cento!" Caesar exclaimed.

"But what if we have to fight. I'm afraid I'll be killed, and my family will never know what happened to me," whimpered Gino.

Stefano, who knew what strength Caesar had, thought he would help reinforce his message. "This is just a resupply run guys, if we watch each other's back and take care of each other, we will make it out of there and be back here to camp before you know it."

Stano chimed in, "No matter what happens to us, let's make a pack that the survivors must make it back home and tell our families what happened and that we were brave in the face of danger." All the boys put their hands into the circle grasping each other and did a group pump handshake.

+++

For the rest of the week nothing changed. They did as they were told and continued to drill. They knew in three days they would be heading to the front-lines of Monfalcone.

After their small meal for dinner, the ones who would be going to the front assembled in a supply tent and were given additional field packs, which consisted of rounds of ammunition, hand grenades, a hunting knife, and a gas mask. Mustard gas was new to the theater, thanks to the Germans. Many countries were finding it an effective way to instantly kill their enemies.

At nighttime while lying in bed, Caesar, like all the other boys, dreamed of home, their families, the smell of their mother's cooking, and of course, their girlfriends or loved ones. All Caesar could see when he

closed his eyes was the smiling face of Generosa looking back at him affectionately with her beautiful blue
eyes.

He thought of the day at Angelo's Café when they
had their photograph taken and how she kissed him
on his cheek. The ache in his heart would pang once
again. The tightness in his gut got worse, and the pain
increased when he thought, *What if I never make it
home?*

10

The Search Continues

Weeks turned into months and months turned into a year. No matter how many times Giuliano and the other families went to the policia, there were no updates. The news from The Front and from what they could gather from the local newspapers was the fighting was intense, but Italy was winning the war. There were no mentions of casualties. Giuliano, Teresa, and the other families never gave up hope. Teresa went to church each day with her sister-in-law, prayed, and lit candles. Their local priest would spend time with them after Mass and try to console them as much as possible.

Every month Generosa would take the family horse and go to visit Giuliano and Teresa. They would sit outside in the warming sun, talk about Caesar, and pray. Teresa knew how much Generosa hurt, losing the love of her life. All she had to do was look over at Giuliano and imagine how she would feel if he was gone, out of her life.

While they were sitting one sunny afternoon, under a shady tree overlooking the fields, Teresa commented that today would be Caesar's eighteenth birthday. They put a candle on a muffin, and Generosa blew out the flame. With sadness in her eyes, Teresa excused herself and went into the house. She came out holding an envelope wrapped in cloth in her hand. She handed it to Generosa.

"I was going through some of Caesar's belongings, while sitting on the edge of his bed praying for his return, when I noticed this yellow envelope under some of his books. I forgot all about it. This is the photograph he shared with me of the two of you at Angleo's on that wonderful day. It's sad he never had a chance to show you."

As Generosa slowly opened the envelope, tears started rolling down her cheeks. Her shoulders started to heave up and down. It was the picture of her and Caesar at the café with the espresso machine in the background. She looked at Teresa and broke down, falling into Teresa's bosom. Teresa just held onto her to comfort her.

"Oh, Signora Buttieri, I don't know what to say. You have given me an incredible gift, one I will cherish forever."

"I hope it makes you feel closer to my son."

"He will always be a part of me," Generosa said in return. Tears continued to well up in her eyes.

+ + +

Each time Generosa and her papa came to visit, Teresa would take Generosa by the hand, and they would walk around the property as Teresa recounted the things Caesar did as a little boy.

"This is where he would play make-believe that he was a knight in shining amour trying to save the princess from the mean dragon."

Generosa started to cry and said, "But he did save the princess from the dragon, when I fell in love with him."

"I could tell he was in love with you Generosa...every time I mentioned your name or said he should start courting you, he would blush, his cheeks would get bright red, and say you two were just friends. But a mother knows these things."

"You are always welcomed in our home Generosa; I think of you as a daughter (*figlia*)." They hugged and cried.

+ + +

Generosa never gave up hope that one day Caesar would return to his family and her. She was now sixteen. Her parents insisted she move on with her life, find a nice man, get married and have children. Generosa just couldn't. At night she would lie awake crying out to Caesar, asking him to let her know he was OK. She prayed to God, said her rosaries, prayed to Jesus and the Blessed Mother. However, her prayers up until this point had not been answered.

To keep herself busy, Generosa decided to get a job working at a local café and bakery in Renazzo, called Novella's Café. She was offered a job at Angelo's, by her uncle, where she and Caesar had their picture taken. But she knew it would just be too hard working there as each time she passed the café stools, it would bring back too much heartbreak and tears.

She loved working, as it kept her busy and her mind occupied, that was until late at night when she was in her bed when she could think of Caesar uninterrupted. A smile would come to her face, she imagined her wedding day with him, how special it would be. Having children together. Growing old together, laughing...and then she would cry herself to sleep.

About once a month when they came to Renazzo, Giuliano and Teresa would stop by Novella's Café and have an espresso or a sandwich, usually mortadella with provolone toasted on pane. Generosa would introduce them as her "in-laws." Even though it made them feel sad, they all smiled knowing they were keeping Caesar's memory alive.

+++

Generosa's parents were very fond of Caesar and had hoped the two of them would marry someday and have a family; but without a word on his whereabouts for over a year, they could only assume the worst. Though they would never say that to Generosa.

Her father would invite young men to the house under the guise to buy some hemp stocks or vegetables from his fields and would then call Generosa out into the yard, where he would introduce her to many fine young men. She showed absolutely no interest. She would tell her mama and papa her heart was already taken.

"Generosa, you must find a nice boy and get married and have children," Her father insisted.

"It would be nice to meet someone, someone who can take care of you," added her mama.

Generosa was furious. "I don't need anyone to take care of me! You raised me to be a strong independent woman, and I am. If Caesar never makes it home, then I will be with him when we are both in Heaven." She stomped out of the room and went outside.

+++

As they entered year two of Caesar being taken, it was now 1917. Giuliano would still visit the local police station a few times a month to see if they had any word about him. There was a list of those who were identified as being "killed in action." His father would read the list every time he stopped by. He never saw Caesar's name on it.

Giuliano just hung his head and cried. He was so full of mixed emotions, from anger at his government, heartache for losing such a wonderful son to the army, and worry that he and Teresa would never see him grow up, marry, and have children. He went outside and sat on the wooden bench and just wept. After about an hour, he finally found the energy to get up from the bench. He dried his eyes and headed home.

+++

A few days later Luciano and Generosa drove their wagon to see Giuliano and Teresa. When they came out of their house, they were pleased to see them and invited them in for some cold lemonade and something to eat.

"Any word Giuliano?" asked Luciano.

"No, nothing. I go to the police station a few times a month now and no word. I even check the list of those killed and his name was not on there." Deep down they all knew since the boys were taken against their will, there probably would be no record of their names.

Teresa went over to Generosa and put her hands on her shoulders, leaned down, and hugged her. Generosa began to weep and said, "Someday I will see my Caesar again. I will never give up hope."

11

The Battle of Battles (1917)

It was an overcast, humid August morning as the 5:00 a.m. bugle woke the boys up like a bomb exploding outside their tent. No one slept well. Caesar could hear his friends tossing and turning all night, along with himself. He thought maybe this time when he awoke, he'd be back in his bedroom, with Gatto at his feet, smelling the sweet aromas coming from his mama's kitchen, as if waking from a bad dream. It wouldn't be the case.

They all popped their heads up from under their blankets and looked at each other. Caesar could see the fear on their faces. He could only imagine what his face looked like. They got dressed in silence and headed to the mess tent for their last breakfast at this camp, at least for a while. Before they left, the boys presented Caesar with a sweet roll and sang Happy Birthday to him. He was now eighteen years old.

They all stood in a circle in the tent and said some prayers. "Please God, watch over us and protect us from any harm...please return us to our families safe and sound," Caesar whispered. A chorus of "Amen" ended the prayer.

On their way to the mess tent, not much was said. They were quiet because they had no idea what came next, because they had no idea what was going to happen. All they knew was they were going to the front where the battle raged and that weighed heavily on their minds.

After breakfast, Benito Mussolini led a group of about two dozen young men over to the transport supply area and instructed them to start loading the horse-drawn wagons and transport motorized vehicles with fresh supplies of food, personal supplies, first-aid kits, jugs of water, ammunition, mortar shells, rifles, machine guns, and machine gun parts. They were all in a line and just kept passing the supplies from one man to another until the wagons and vehicles were full. A tarp was laid over the backs of the wagons and tightened down for the three-plus hour ride. There were six wagons in total and three transport vehicles. Three Fiat 2000 tanks led the procession.

Caesar, Stefano, Gino, and Stano stepped up into one of the wagons, with a sergeant driving the team of horses. The other young men went where they were instructed. In the lead transport vehicle was Benito Mussolini.

The caravan drove past small rural towns on its way to the encampment at Monfalcone. The ride was bumpy, hot, and dusty on a mid-August afternoon, and long. As they got closer to the frontline, they could hear the sounds of war: bombs and mortar rounds going off and planes buzzing in the air. As they pulled into the frontline base, Caesar and his group dismounted from the wagons and trucks and stood in formation. They were instructed to unload the supplies and follow the regulars who had been at this out-post for the last six-months to show them where to stack everything. Caesar noticed that this encamp-ment was much larger than the one he came from, as this group consisted of over 5000 fighting men and about 200 others consisting of medical personnel, cooks, and helpers. These men came from the various mini-encampments around the region.

Once the supplies were unloaded, the wagons and trucks were loaded with empty crates and boxes for the ride back to the Portogruaro camp. They would make this same trip once a week for the next three months.

After their last supply run, when they got back to their base, they all assembled in the mess tent. While they were eating, the superiors came in and an-nounced the Austrians had opened up some new fronts, flanking to San Giovanni di Duino. On their next trip up to Monfalcone, they would be staying up in that area to help support and fill in for the 750 men who would be sent to Duino. The boys all shot their heads up and looked at each other in fear. Caesar gave them all a stern look as if saying, *Stay strong, do not show weakness in here.*

They also announced another platoon of soldiers would be going to Caporetto, just north of Monfalcone to engage in the Isonzo Campaign. (These forces would include Benito Mussolini.)

The next morning after waking and putting on their uniforms, they again said a prayer. This one was simple and to the point, led by Stefano, "Dear Lord, watch over us and protect us from any harm," A quick "Amen" resonated throughout the tent.

As they made their way to the mess tent, they noticed several transport vehicles pulling into the camp. These vehicles were filled with replacements—about 200 young men in total.

+++

After breakfast the loaded caravan made its way, once again, east to Monfalcone. This time there were over 250 men marching north. Just like two weeks ago, as they got closer, the sounds of war became louder. This caravan consisted of seven wagons, four transport vehicles dragging cannons behind them, and four Fiat tanks. They were only a few miles from the Monfalcone camp when all of a sudden, loud explosions erupted all around them. Several sergeants yelled, "Cover!" as men dove under the wagons and many scattered into the woods. The mortar rounds landed all over. One made a direct hit on a wagon full of food supplies, demolishing the wagon, and killing two horses. Several men walking next to the wagon were blown to bits. Body parts flew through the air and excruciating screams could be heard all over.

Caesar, Stefano, Gino, and Stano were trailing the wagon behind the one that was hit. The concussion from the explosion knocked them to the ground. They were stunned, their ears ringing. As soon as they came to their senses they ducked and took cover. Their heads were swiveling left and right waiting for the next mortars to explode. Stefano looked down at his side and saw a couple of blown-up legs with the boots still on and several bloodied severed hands near his foot. His stomach turned and he vomited.

The men in charge instructed some of the soldiers to fire mortars back in the direction from where they came. After several barrages of mortar fire, the air was thick. The smell of sulfur, smoke, and death were in the air. They must have hit their targets and driven the Austrians back.

After waiting about fifteen-minutes, they all got back on their feet, secured the wagons, and continued their short journey to Monfalcone. When they arrived, they unloaded their supplies and those who were wounded from the mortar attacks were sent to the casualty tents to be taken care of.

+++

The next morning Lieutenant Carpilio assembled two groups of young men to perform small reconnaissance missions near San Giovanni di Duino, where the new front had opened, to uncover their enemy's troop strengths and the amount of heavy weaponry they may possess. They all climbed onto the three horse-drawn wagons for the short ride from Monfalcone to Duino. They were all frightened.

When they arrived, they all climbed down from the wagons and filed in formation. Lieutenant Carpilio broke out the groups into two. Group A, were instructed to go "sweep" the upper woods for signs of the Austrian troops, and if confronted, engage the enemy. Shoot to kill orders were given.

Group B consisted of Caesar, Stefano, Gino, Stano, and eight other boys. They were led by Corporal Antonelli. When they got to the small clearing, they swept the area to make sure no Austrian soldiers were nearby. They were scared and anxious about what might happen.

They walked over and looked down the grassy embankment that led to the edge of a river about 100 yards below. The hill had a pretty steep drop-off and the bottom of the hill to the water's edge was about a two-foot embankment to the river.

It was a clear sunny day, which made it easy for them to see across the river to the other side to ensure that no enemy troops were lying in wait for them. Though the sun did cause a bit of a glare bouncing off the water.

The guys spread out in a line of defense at the top of the hill as they descended to the river below. They kept about fifty yards apart from each other, close enough that if something happened, they would be able to respond in time. Caesar was in the middle, Gino and Stano were to his right, and Stefano was to his left. The other young men flanked behind to cover their backs. They were all carrying their Vetterli rifles with bayonets attached, ready for action.

As they slowly descended the hill about fifty yards, Caesar was signaling to Corporal Antonelli that he was moving more towards his left, closer to Stefano. Stefano looked over and gave Caesar a nod. Conversation or orders given were delivered with hand or head signals to avoid sounds that could alert the enemy. As Stefano reached the bottom of the bank, he looked over at Caesar and gave the thumbs up. Corporal Antonelli turned and waved the second row of young men to proceed down the bank, but to keep an eye out behind them to avert any kind of ambush from above.

As Caesar drew closer to Stefano, he saw a movement just to the left side of Stefano near the water. He wasn't sure what it was. There was a large rock formation that stuck out into the river that blocked Caesar's complete view from around the other side of the rock. But he knew he saw something glimmering off the water. Was it the sunlight reflecting off the water, or as his mind raced, was it maybe the barrel of a rifle?

As he was about to signal something to Stefano, Caesar saw the water create a wake from behind the rock formation that rolled in front of Stefano and him. Before Caesar could alert Stefano, four Austrian soldiers waded around the corner of the rock edge that jutted out into the river. They were knee deep in the water. They were all young, and from the crispness of their uniforms, new to this war. They were so close in proximity, all six of them had a look of surprise and fear on their faces at the same time. They all froze.

Caesar seemed to be the first to shake out of his stupor and realized he had the advantage of being above them on the down slope of the hill. The four Austrian soldiers had to adjust for any uphill angle shot or attack. They were not quick enough. Caesar didn't hesitate, survival instincts kicked in...flight or fight...not Caesar...it was fight.

In his sloped position, Caesar discharged his single-bolt rifle at the first soldiers' chest and fired. The soldier dropped into the river, both hands gripping his chest, screaming in pain while blood began to float on the top of the water. The screams distracted the other three soldiers who looked at their comrade floating face up in the river; he fell silent.

One of the other Austrian soldiers quickly lifted his rifle at Stefano and fired, hitting him in the left shoulder, he fell backwards to the ground in pain. He quickly grabbed his shoulder as blood oozed through his clasped hand. Caesar ran over and knelt next to him to check on his wound. As he did, another Austrian soldier fired, hitting Caesar in the upper thigh of his leg. Blood leaked out as he grabbed his thigh in pain, but he ignored the pain and stood up, knowing they were still in a dangerous situation.

The sound of gunfire and screams alerted Gino, Stano, Corporal Antonelli and the others, who waved the other soldiers to engage the Austrians. Though they hesitated to fire their rifles because Caesar and Stefano were between them and the enemy.

The three remaining Austrian soldiers rushed at Stefano and Caesar. As the soldiers started to climb the two-foot embankment out of the water, Stefano cocked his rifle while on his back and fired. He hit one soldier in the stomach, who fell backwards into the river with a big splash. He too floated on the water, dead. Stefano struggled to sit up to give himself a better advantage.

By now the two remaining Austrian soldiers and Caesar and Stefano were only a few feet from each other. Caesar stood and squared himself, aimed, and fired his rifle at the soldier, but nothing happened. His rifle had jammed. *Oh no! Now what?* he thought.

But before Caesar could angle his bayonet to use, he felt the cold steel of a blade slicing through his ribs. He lost his breath, his legs began to give way as he staggered a little to his left, then to his right, and he dropped to his knees. Caesar gasped, as dark red blood spilled out his left side and mouth. He grabbed his side and tried to apply pressure. The pain was unbearable. As he looked up, the soldier was preparing to stab Caesar a second time with his bayonet leading the way.

Gino and Stano began to close ground, running as fast as they could towards them. Gino had looked on watching as the Austrian soldier plunged his bayonet into the side of Caesar. Gino, now had a better angle, raised his rifle and fired; his bullet blew half of the Austrian soldier's face off before he could stab again. There was only one remaining Austrian soldier. Before Gino or Stano could engage their next bullet, the Austrian soldier took his bayonet and plunged it into the stomach of Stefano as he sat on the ground to try and finish him off. Stefano screamed in agony as blood seeped out of his uniform. As the soldier went to stab Stefano a second time, Caesar found what little energy he had left and from his kneeling position, thrust his bayonet into the Austrian soldier's gut. Pulled it out with great effort and pain, then thrust again. As the soldier staggered backwards, another shot rang out. The bullet pierced the heart of the soldier. It was Stano! The soldier fell backwards in the grass, taking Caesar's rifle embedded in his belly with him. He was dead!

Stefano looked over in agony at Caesar and said, "You saved my life!" By this time Gino and Stano dropped to their knees near their friends. Corporal Antonelli instructed the other soldiers to slowly go around the rock formation to see if there were any more Austrian soldiers on the other side.

Caesar looked at his friends and said, "Well, we stuck together my friends (*i miei amici*)." He was still on his knees, blood dribbling out of his mouth and wetting the side of his uniform where the bayonet had penetrated. His arms dangled down to his side, and then as if in slow motion, his eyes closed, head and chin slumped down against his chest. Gino frantically broke out his medical kit and started applying large clumps of cotton and old rags to Caesar and Stefano's wounds. Red liquid continued flowing from Caesar's mouth. Stefano, Gino, and Stano were in a state of shock. "No, no, Caesar you cannot die!"

They kept yelling his name and saying, "Don't die my friend!" (*Non morire mio amico!*)

With Caesar's last breath, he looked up at his friends with faded glassy eyes and said, "Tell Generosa, I will always love her...I will always be with her." With that, he slumped forward, face down in the grass. Caesar was dead.

Stano, Stefano, and Gino were in total shock and distraught as they held onto their friend's lifeless body crying. All of a sudden, a strange blue light engulfed Caesar, like a warm blanket. The three of them looked at each other in amazement.

Stefano bowed his head in prayer and wept openly and said, "God has taken him home."

+++

Someone brought down two large blankets for Stano and Gino to wrap Caesar's lifeless body in, to bring back to camp. Another helped Stefano up the hill to the wagon. Once back at their camp at Portogruaro, Stano and Gino carried his body to the makeshift morgue for a doctor to confirm death.

The next day, Stano and Gino would carry Caesar's body into the woods to bury, but instead of him being placed in the makeshift graves where the other deceased soldiers were buried, they decided he deserved to be buried by himself. After digging his grave, gently placing his wrapped body inside, and filling it back in, they placed a handmade cross at his head and said a prayer. Stano carved CB into the cross.

About a week later when Stefano got out of the field hospital, Gino and Stano walked him over to show where Caesar was buried. Not a word was said, only tears and sniffles from the three friends.

Reality set in. They realized they had lost their friend, their leader, and their inspiration. Stefano told Gino and Stano because of his injuries he would be going home soon, and he would tell Caesar's family and Generosa what happened. "We owe him that much."

Caesar was now safe and at peace.

+++

A few days later, a group was assembled by Corporal Antonelli, which included Gino, Stano, and four other young soldiers. They were offloading some of the munitions and mortar rounds that had just arrived from Padua. They would need to take inventory today before heading back to the frontlines with another resupply mission.

Suddenly, a crate of mortar rounds that Stano and Gino were carrying slipped from their hands. They both looked at each other in horror as the crate crashed and splintered as it hit the hard ground. They both started to run as if the crate would explode. But nothing happened. Antonelli spewed a few profanities. "Phew that was close," Stano said, as he looked over at the crate. Several mortar shells had rolled out onto the ground. Before Stano, Gino, and others knew what happened two shells exploded. The blast blew them all back about thirty feet. The other soldiers scattered. Gino sustained shrapnel wounds to his left leg, knocking him to the ground. Stano took the blast to his head as he flew through the air. He hit the ground hard but was moving. Another soldier was killed. The other soldiers nearby quickly carried the injured into the field hospital tent.

After two weeks in the infirmary, Stano and Gino were released from the hospital and from their military duties. Like Stefano, they were being sent home. Though they longed to get home to their families, Stefano, Gino, and Stano just wept, knowing their friend, protector and mentor was not coming home with them, alive. Stefano asked and was given permission by the camp General to allow them to bring the body of Caesar back home. Gino, who was a good woodworker, built a makeshift, roughhewn coffin from the poplar trees in the woods.

+++

(An aside.) Benito Mussolini would fight valiantly in Carporetto during the Isonzo Campaign and ascend to the rank of corporal because of his tenacity, grit, and fearless leadership. He too would be wounded by a mortar shell and would eventually be sent home in 1917. He would go on to establish a pro-war propagandist newspaper called *Il Popolo d'Italia* in Milan. He would start a political movement and take over Italy and establish a fascist government and propel Italy into an alliance with Germany and into World War II.

12

Caesar Comes Home (1917)

The day came when Stefano, Gino, and Stano would be coming home due to their injuries. Stefano would always have a limp as the bayonet severed a couple nerves near his spine. Gino would need a cane to walk with from the shrapnel blast to his leg, and Stano, who sustained head trauma from the blast, would struggle with his coordination and memory.

They uncovered the grave and carried the hand-made coffin out of the woods and with the help of some of the other young men, who had looked up to Caesar. They helped place him in a sturdier coffin then used extra burlap bags to cover the body and the smell. They threw some lime powder into the coffin and sealed it up.

The three boys, now young men, climbed up onto the wagon, with Caesar's coffin in the back and took the slow ride to the Portogruaro train station. Though there was seating up front, the three never left Caesar's side as his coffin was placed at the rear of the train. Within a few hours the train pulled into Ferrara. The three of them looked at each other, and they all embraced.

"Well Caesar, we have arrived in Ferrara, now it's time to take you home my friend," said Stefano between sniffles.

Gino went to ask a local farmer if they could borrow his wagon and horse. After hearing their story, he gave the wagon to them with pride and even supplied them with food and water. They carried the coffin to the wagon and tied it down, then standing there, said a few prayers, Afterwards, they got up into the wagon. Stefano took the reins and snapped the horse into action.

The ride back was quiet, the three young men silently replaying the last year and a half in their minds...was it all a bad dream? In unison, they looked over their shoulders at the coffin carrying Caesar. They had their answer.

When they rode through the town of San Venanzio, they knew they were close to Caesar's house. They stopped just up the street and looked at each other.

"Even though this has been the most tragic of events in our lives my friends, I am glad we journeyed this road together," whispered Stefano.

"It would have been a sin to leave our Caesar back there in a grave in the woods," Gino chimed in, "but he is home now, where he belongs and where he is loved."

They decided just to ride into the front yard and explain everything to Signore and Signora Buttieri. They took a deep breath and continued the one-mile trip down the road.

As they got closer, they saw a dog running at full speed toward them. It was Gatto. He kept running around the wagon, jumping and whimpering. They stopped. Instinctively, Gatto jumped up on the back of the wagon, and he sadly lay across the coffin. He was protecting his Caesar for the rest of the ride.

As they pulled into the yard, they saw several people chatting, sitting at a long wooden table beneath the trees. Every head looked over at the wagon as they pulled to a stop. Stefano instantly noticed Generosa and her papa. Giuliano stood up quickly, recognizing the boys but with a confused look on his face. He bolted over to the wagon. Stefano slowly descended and embraced Giuliano, both in tears.

Giuliano looked at the three boys in their military uniforms and kept looking past them for Caesar. Just as Giuliano was going to ask where Caesar was, he saw the coffin in the back of the wagon with Gatto draped over it whimpering. He and Stefano locked eyes and Stefano just nodded yes. Giuliano's worst fears were realized, he fell to his knees weeping.

Teresa and Generosa came running over and stared in disbelieve at the coffin. They knew what was happening. Generosa scrambled up on the back of the wagon and along with Gatto draped herself over his coffin. Through tears and sobbing she said, "*Amore mio, amore mio, sei tornato a casa.*" (My love, my love, you've come home.)

A distraught Giuliano escorted the boys to the table. Everyone sat down and wanted to know the whole story. Before he could start, Generosa said through tears, "Can you tell me how my Caesar died?"

Stefano hesitated, he looked down with tears in his eyes and said, "Generosa, I would rather tell you how he lived, how he saved our lives and the lives of many others, and what a hero he was."

+++

The war ended November 4, 1918, with the signing of the Armistice of Villa Giusti. It was signed near Padua, Italy, and ended military operations on the Italian Front.

(A side note.) After the war was won, Italy received less than she had been promised in the Treaty of London, much less than what Italians regarded as their country's due. The population gained by the acquisition of the northern Italian territories won back, were about the same as Italy's wartime casualties. About five-and-a-half-million men entered the services, and of these, two-fifths became casualties, about 689,000 killed, and about one million seriously wounded. The economy had expanded, but Italy was left with massive international debt. All of these factors contributed to the rise of fascism only a few years later.

Part II

Plymouth, Massachusetts

13

Plymouth, the Early Years

Plymouth, Massachusetts–1970

M arie was born into a modest family of three in "America's Hometown" of Plymouth, Massachusetts; about forty-five miles south of Boston. She was the daughter of Donato and Betty Ann Buttieri. Her dad was a second-generation Italian, and her mom was of English descent, tracing her heritage back to the Pilgrims and the Mayflower crossing. Her father, aside from being an exceptional athlete and an above average baseball player, was the town's barber, and her mom worked at the local grade school cafeteria.

Marie was spoiled by everyone in her family. In fact, the day she was born, her father, unknown to her mother, closed his barbershop and went around town visiting his friends with a bottle of Sambuca to celebrate his little girl. Donato's smile beamed from one side of his mouth to the other throughout the day, almost in a permanent grin.

At five-years old, she stood about three-and-a-half feet tall, wiry with light skin, short black hair in a Dutch cut, with bangs accenting her big brown eyes, a mischievous smile, and lots of freckles.

When she got a little older, she complained to her mother, "Mom, how come I got so many freckles?"

Her mom, being the wonderful mother she was, said with a smile, "Angels give out freckles to their favorite little girls...so you must have lots of angels keeping an eye on you."

Marie gave her mother the "Marie look" (a scrunched-up face with squinted eyes), as if only half believing what her mother was telling her. Her mom just smiled at her and added, "Don't make that face for too long, or it may freeze that way."

Marie just looked at her mom and crossed her arms with a loud, "Humph!"

As she got older, she would tell her dad to keep her hair short so she could play sports. She was a bit of a tomboy and a great little athlete. By the time she turned nine, she was a regular beach goer with her family at Plymouth Long Beach, just offshore from the Plymouth Waterfront. She loved the sun, playing kickball and wiffle ball on the beach with her friends, and now had her new little brother Michael to play with in the water, who had just turned two. Though most people called him Mickey.

+ + +

Long Beach is a three-mile stretch of beautiful beaches on the oceanside with hundreds of large boulders and rocks on the east side bracing the peninsula from massive storms. This man-made seawall also helped to reduce beach erosion and road washouts. About a half-mile out from the Plymouth waterfront,

Long Beach's sand dunes and vegetation cascaded across the inner harbor like a Norman Rockwell painting. It can range in width between 50 and 100 yards depending on high sea erosion from that year's storms.

Long Beach acts as a barrier peninsula protecting this quaint historic waterfront. Especially during nor'easters, ocean storms, and hurricanes. A smattering of cottages polka-dot the harborside, overlooking the seaport village of Plymouth, like sentries lending a watchful eye. The houses all sit on stilts so during high ocean tides, or the crashing waves from storms, the water flows under the houses rather than damaging their foundations.

+++

Like most families in Plymouth in the 60s and 70s, Marie's Italian grandmother, Noni, moved in with her and her family after her husband, Antonio (or Nino as most called him) had passed away from cancer. Though everyone called her Noni, Marie more times than not, called her grandmother by her first name...*Ida*, not out of disrespect, but out of pure unconditional love and joy for "her" little Ida.

Noni stood about five foot two, with a beautiful round cherub face, a larger-than-life smile, and a joyful demeanor. Her silvery hair matched her hazel eyes. She loved to wear bold red lipstick and always made sure to look fashionable.

She was one of four sisters, who did not have it easy when her parents first moved to Plymouth from Sant'Agostino, Italy. She was a very hard worker, resolute, and cherished her husband Nino, her son Donato, his wife Betty Ann, their children Marie and Mickey. Family and God were a big part of her life.

14

The Italian Migration

Nino and Ida were both born and grew up in Plymouth after their families emigrated in the early 1900s from the Bologna area, which included Cento, Renazzo, and Sant'Agostino areas of Italy. Their desire was to provide a better life for themselves and eventually for their children. Ida had three sisters: Julia, Florence, and Dolores, though everyone called her Dolly. Their parents were Argia and Igino Maini. They were all humble and God-fearing Catholics. They went to Mass daily to give God thanks and to pray for everyone they knew. Noni was the great-niece of Generosa Trocchi.

When the sisters were in their teens their father, Igino, got sick. He died young, presumably of a stomach condition, that today might be attributed to stomach cancer.

Their mother, Argia, could not speak much English so it was hard for her to find a fulltime job. However, she, like many recent Italian immigrants, found odd jobs to do in the area, from sewing to cleaning houses. One place she also helped clean was the Plymouth Cordage Company. Her four girls were expected to help bring in some extra money to make ends meet. At their young age, they also worked at odd jobs around the neighborhood: cleaning houses, helping local stores fill their shelves, even picking blueberries for five cents a pint.

Every day either before or after school they would tend to their various jobs. When they got home, they would hand over the coins they earned that day to their mother. Argia would take their coins to make sure she had enough to put towards the rent, food, and other essential provisions. Then looking upon her four girls, handed them back a few pennies...they beamed with delight!

Nino had nine brothers and sisters. He and a few of his brothers all worked at "the Cordage," as everyone in town called it. Nino was a local baseball standout. He was the great-nephew of Giuliano Buttieri.

+++

Most of the Italians who emigrated to the Plymouth area from Bologna, Cento, and Renazzo in the early 1900s found work making rope and twine at the Plymouth Cordage Company in North Plymouth. Their skills as hemp farmers back in Italy, gave them a leg up when starting with the company.

The Plymouth Cordage Company was established in 1824 by Bourne Spooner, a descendant of several Pilgrim families. After securing investments from others, they constructed their factory on the Plymouth waterfront in North Plymouth, which features a deep natural harbor that allowed large ships to dock with ease.

The Plymouth Cordage Company had a philosophy that was far-reaching for its time. The company offered far more than factory jobs. They provided housing and medical facilities, a school, and library. To keep workers happy (a major thrust of their philosophy), they also offered places for social and physical activities including a gymnasium, bowling alley, and a Men's club. You'll find many of the houses they built then still in use today.[xi]

While it ceased operation in 1964, the Plymouth Cordage Company served as the largest employer in Plymouth for over 100 years after operating continuously for over 140 years.

+ + +

Nino had two loves...his Ida and baseball. During the early evenings and on weekends, you could find him at the local baseball field. He was a cut above everyone else. You could say he was a natural. He stood about five foot six, was lean and solid. He kept his black hair short and parted down the middle. He could run like the wind and was tenacious. He played third base for the Plymouth Town Team. He loved the "hot corner," and would face down any baseball hit towards him and had the broken fingers to prove it.

Nino's reputation as an exceptional ballplayer got around, and scouts from some of the semi-pro teams started to show up at his games. He was fearless, he was fast and had a great bat. He even used his body when needed to knock a ball down and throw the runner out, even the fastest runners, often by a few steps. The talk around town was he had the talent to go to the pros. The big dance!

When he was around eighteen years old, he strived to fulfill his dream of becoming a professional baseball player. The following spring of 1937 he received a letter asking him to try out for the St. Louis Cardinals baseball team. Everyone in the family was so excited.

A few days later, he was home nursing a hamstring pull he incurred from an earlier ballgame. He was outside mowing his mother's lawn with a push mower...no power mowers back in those days. A couple of guys approached him from the ballfield down the street and said they needed an umpire because the original ump couldn't make it to the game.

Nino hesitated because his coach told him to rest his leg for the upcoming game. Even Ida told him he shouldn't go. She would later say she had a premonition that something might happen. But Nino couldn't let the other ballplayers down. That's just how he was.

So, he walked down to the ballfield. As the team in the field was warming up, Nino yelled out to toss the balls in, so they could start the game. One guy didn't quite get the message and threw the ball in hard just as Nino turned and the ball hit him square in the right eye. He dropped to the ground like a sack of potatoes. He would spend the next two weeks in the hospital and to his dismay, the doctors told him he would never regain sight in that one eye. If his accident had happened today, the doctors could easily have saved his eye.

The bad news crushed him, his family, and friends. Losing his eye extinguished one of his true dreams...to be a major league baseball player. If he hadn't lost his eye...he had a great chance of making it to the major leagues. Though to the surprise of many, he never lost his sense of humor or optimism.

With his job prospects limited in Plymouth because of the loss of his eye, he found a good paying job at Wheeler Reflector Company a few towns away in Hanson, Massachusetts. They produced light bulbs and light fixtures of all sizes.

Hanson was about twenty minutes northeast of Plymouth. The town's claim to fame then: It was the original home of the Ocean Spray Cranberry Company.

Since he and Ida were planning on getting married, he also needed to find a home fitting for his new bride to be. He found such a house on Reed Street in Hanson, about a five-minute walk from his new employer.

After visiting the house, he rushed back to Plymouth to tell Ida he had found the perfect home for them. She was so excited about their new life. They jumped into his old jalopy and headed up to Hanson.

When they arrived at the house, Nino had forgotten to tell Ida how much work the house needed. He kept mentioning that her brothers-in-law and his friend Giamarco would help him repair the roof, the windows, and pour concrete over the dirt floor in the basement.

As Ida walked around inside the house, she asked, "But where is the toilet?"

Nino immediately deflected and said pointing out the window, "See the big backyard. We could put in a large vegetable garden."

Looking out the back window, she spotted it...in the corner of the lot, off the back of the house to the left, a small rectangular shaped building...she looked up at him and said with a hint of skepticism, "What's that?"

"Um...ah...that's the outhouse?" He squeaked out.

Ida's face got red. "If you think you are going to marry me, and bring me to this house with no indoor toilet, you better think twice mister!" she exclaimed.

They were married in early 1942, and when they entered their home, there was a new indoor toilet!

+++

Later that year Ida gave birth to their only child, a baby boy they named Donato.

Nino continued to go to work every day at Wheeler Reflector and would walk home at noon to have lunch with his wife and his baby boy. He couldn't get enough of his little boy. It didn't take Nino long to get Donato a baseball glove and teach him the game he loved. They were inseparable. At about the age of five, during his lunch breaks, Nino would toss a baseball with his son and teach him how to swing a bat. Donato got the bug! He even slept with his glove at night.

As Donato grew up and went to the local high school, he too was becoming an outstanding baseball player. He was a natural lefty hitter and was fast on his feet and had an uncanny quick ball reaction in left field.

In 1959, Donato, now seventeen, was playing baseball for the Hanson Town Team against Plymouth. His father, Nino, was the coach. He played against some of his cousins who played for Plymouth.

These games were big local attractions, and fans filled up the Siever Field stands and along the sides of the field. It was also known as The Dump, as it was a dumping ground in the past for The Cordage Company. During the games a tin cup was passed around for any donations to help support the league. Hanson won seven to six in a tight, hard fought match.

At the end of the game, he caught the attention of a young lady sitting in the stands with her friends. He couldn't keep his eyes off of her. He saw one of his cousins talking to the girls, so he walked over and introduced himself. Her name was Betty Ann. After a couple years of dating, they got engaged.

Donato was torn between his love of baseball and his new bride to be. He was talented enough to try out for a professional baseball team, but it would mean moving out of the area and away from his and Betty Ann's families.

He wanted to be a barber and had been working as an intern for his father's brother, Joe, who had a barbershop in North Plymouth. When his uncle offered him a fulltime job with the prospect of taking over the shop upon his retirement, Donato jumped at the chance. His dream of raising a family was stronger than baseball.

Knowing he would have to move to Plymouth, he started looking around the area and with the help of his mother and dad, he found a nice home on Olmstead Terrace. It was a beautiful two-story red brick house, with white trim, a large picture window overlooking the street, and a two-car garage under the house with a semi-circular driveway. Before he put an offer in on the house, he brought Betty Ann over to look at the house. She loved it! They got engaged in 1963 and married in 1964. Early the following year, Marie was born.

On weekends, they would drive to Hanson to his parents' house for dinners or cookouts. Nino, now called Gramp, and Ida just doted over little Marie and couldn't get enough.

15

Marie Grows Up (1981)

At sixteen, Marie was a happy-go-lucky young woman with a big heart and as they say, "Someone who would give you the shirt off her back." But like everyone, she had her share of ups and downs. As a teenager attending Plymouth-Carver High School, she was an exceptional athlete, excelling in field hockey and softball, but her grades were just average. She didn't have her eye on college, she just wanted to follow her passion of baking and cooking and keeping those around her happy and content. That was Marie.

She started dating Anthony in their sophomore year of high school. Most people called him Tony. She preferred Anthony. They had met in grade school, but were never in each other's classes, so they rarely saw one another.

Tony was a strapping young man, about five foot eleven with natural muscles, which he got not just from working out, but also from working on his dad's forty-foot commercial fishing boat. He had brown eyes and shoulder length brown hair that he kept in place with his faded red bandana.

He was an exceptional athlete and the starting quarterback for the Plymouth-Carver Eagles. Sports came easily to him, and he relished the success he was having on and off the field with his first love, Marie.

He always called her Mia Bella, a term of endearment meaning my beautiful.

A bad knee injury from football, in his senior year, ended his sports career. However, it never kept him from working with the youth in town sports. He helped coach the peewee football and farm league baseball teams. The kids called him "Coach Tony."

Marie would joke with him and say, "Yeah, but I can still beat you in a game of HORSE any day," referring to a basketball shooting contest. The rules are you designate places to shoot from. Every time you sink a basket from one of the spots you get a letter until you sink enough baskets to spell the word H-O-R-S-E. If you miss a basket before spelling horse, your opponent gets to try until they miss. Marie won about 90 percent of the time. Getting beat by a girl used to infuriate Anthony.

They continued to date all through high school and a few years after graduating, they got engaged. A while later, after they were able to save some money, they were married. It was 1985. Anthony was twenty-one and Marie was twenty.

It was a small wedding, just close family, and friends. They wanted to keep it small so they could use as much of the gift money and the money they'd saved to buy a small house in town. They found a quaint three-bedroom, two-bath home on Howland Street just off Court Street in downtown Plymouth.

It was close to the Town Wharf where Anthony's dad docked his commercial fishing boat, and where

Anthony worked along with two of his high school buddies. Their business was good, and they made a decent living on the sea. It wasn't an easy life on the water, especially during the winters. What made it worthwhile was doing what they loved.

+++

Now married, Marie was moving out of her family home on Olmstead Terrace, which meant leaving her little Ida. Though they would only live about a mile away from each other, Marie was still sad to go. Her Noni came into her bedroom while Marie was packing up some clothes and sat at the edge of her bed.

Noni patted a spot next to herself for Marie to sit. Marie went over and sat down. Noni held Marie's hand and gently rubbed it. After a little pause, Noni said, "I can't believe my little girl is now married and moving on to begin a new life. May God bless you, Anthony, and the children you will someday have."

Marie's eyes started to water. "I'm a little scared Ida."

Noni continued, "There will be ups and downs in your marriage, but Anthony is a very good man. He's a hard worker. He loves you very much and will provide for you. The days you have arguments, and they will happen, remember you two are a team now, forgive, forget, and move-on."

Marie wrapped her arms around her with a big bear hug, gave her a big squeeze, lifted her feet off the ground, and lightly swaying her from side-to-side saying, "I love you my little Ida."

Marie grabbed her grandmother's other hand and kissed them both. "You always know what to say, and I will always remember your advice. I will miss you, my little Ida." They hugged and cried.

After drying her eyes, Marie got up and finished packing her boxes of clothes and other items.

"Ida, I will always have this." Marie showed Noni a framed picture of her, Noni, and Gramp at Marie's Confirmation at St. Mary's Church in North Plymouth. Noni smiled a sad smile as she remembered her best friend and late husband.

+++

Over the next few days Marie, Anthony, their family, friends, and parents loaded boxes of clothes, memorabilia, and furniture from both of their homes and made the easy trip to Howland Street. It was like watching an ant colony streaming in and out of their new home. The two of them were so happy. Every time they took a break from moving their household items in, they'd hand everyone a beer and then just look around their new home in awe and start grinning from ear to ear as they hugged each other. Of course that turned into a group hug!

Their house would become the new meeting place for getting together with family and friends. But they always looked forward to the mandatory Sunday dinner with her family on Olmstead Terrace. Lots of homemade pasta with Bolognese sauce, homemade tortellini filled with pork in chicken broth. The crostini horn and gnocch breads, and desserts came from Borsari's bakery in North Plymouth and the Italian slice meats and wine came from Perry's Market. Lots of love, warmth, wine, and hearty laughter.

+++

Marie and Anthony tried having children in the first few years of their marriage, even seeking medical help, but nothing seemed to work. That was OK with her as she had Anthony to keep her happy, and they could always adopt if they wanted to. Her life was full.

+++

Marie continued to work at Borsari Bakery, where she had worked since she was fifteen. Her specialties were making the best desserts, from cannoli to pizzelles, tiramisu, Boston Cream Pie, to her famous biscotti. Her cannoli mix was so famous that old Mrs. Gallerani would always ask if Marie had mixed the cannoli filling for the day's pastries. If she hadn't, Mrs. Gallerani would pass the display case, crinkling up her nose, and order some other pastry.

Marie loved everyone she worked for, from the owners, Mr. and Mrs. Borsari, her co-workers Filomena, Claudia, and Beatrice, and all the customers. This was where she felt Plymouth was like a big family.

Throughout high school Tony continued working on his father's fishing boat, named "The Dream," which reflected what was important in his father's life and that was his family. The plan was after a couple years of his being out of school, Tony and his dad would buy a second boat just for lobstering. This boat would be Tony's with a crew of three of his buddies. Tony loved being on the water. He better; it was a tough job, with pretty much five or six days a week of getting up around 4:30 a.m., casting off ropes by 5:00 a.m., returning to harbor around 4:30 p.m. to unload the day's catch. Somedays would be shorter depending on the weather.

A couple of years later, in 1987, on a beautiful Plymouth waterfront day, the new lobster boat pulled around the Plymouth jetty and docked at Town Wharf. Marie was waiting on the wharf. Tony jumped out and tied the boat up to the docking post. He grabbed Marie's hand and walked her back to the stern of the boat. In large, stenciled letters the words *MIA BELLA* were spelled out.

Marie just looked at Anthony, and her eyes welled up. She hugged him hard and said, "Only you would do something like this, my love, and I just love being your Mia Bella." Tony smiled back and thought to himself...*He done did good!*

16

A Miracle Arrives (1990)

About three years later, one day Marie started feeling sick to her stomach, like a flu bug had hit her. She only felt nauseous, no cold, no stuffiness, or even a fever. It happened off and on for about a couple weeks. Then her body became overly sensitive to touch. Marie just didn't feel like herself. She also realized she had missed her period. She thought to herself, *Could it be? No, it can't be!*

She knew she always prayed to God for a gift...the gift of a child...were her prayers being answered? She reflected on a dream she had as a teenager. Every time she saw a baby in the arms of its mother, her mind would wander and then she would see herself holding that little infant, with the proud momma bear look. She went to her doctor and her dreams were realized. Marie was pregnant. She and Anthony were going to have a baby!

After she left the doctor's office on Chilton Street in downtown Plymouth, she was so excited she ran down to the town wharf to await Anthony's lobster boat, the Mia Bella. His boat usually came into harbor around 4:30 p.m. Plymouth being Plymouth, her doctor's office was one block away from the pier.

It was an overcast day as she saw the boat round the inside turn at Bug Light. It followed the markers into the harbor, past the Long Beach cottages on the left, then cut right around the long stone jetty, past the Portico and dock displaying the famed Plymouth Rock and the Mayflower ship. The Mia Bella chugged up to the town pier to unload their catch of lobsters for the day, she was ecstatic.

It had been a long day at sea for Tony and his crew, as were most days. He was lucky to have such a dedicated group of guys. Back in high school they all played together on the football team and had a strong bond. There wasn't anything they wouldn't do for each other. As they finished hauling in their last pots of the day, he felt a chill in the air and coughed, a dry cough that he had off and on for a few weeks. *It's just the damp weather,* he said to himself.

As Tony looked up from his captain's wheelhouse, he saw Marie running toward him, spastically waving her arms in the air. At first, he thought something was wrong. She looked so frantic, but as she drew closer, he realized she had the biggest smile on her face, that beamed of pure happiness.

What could it be? he thought. He jumped from the boat onto the dock and started running towards her.

"Anthony, Anthony!" Marie yelled in excitement, "We're gonna have a baby!"

+++

Both sides of the family were ecstatic and overjoyed. A new addition, a new link to the past and a purveyor of traditions into the future. A true miracle! Later the following year, Jacelyn Marie was born. Marie liked to call her Jace for short. She was born in September, seven pounds, nineteen inches long. She had a full head of light brown hair, and eventually, big brown eyes, and like her mom, freckles.

The proud parents were beaming with so much joy they couldn't contain their excitement. Tears fell from not only the eyes of the assembled family and friends, but also Anthony's. Marie stepped next to Anthony and they both embraced.

They both looked at each other and said in unison, "There's our little angel!"

Marie couldn't wait to place Jacelyn into the arms of her parents. Both Donato and Betty Ann had been praying for a grandchild. Of course, Donato was praying for a little boy so he could teach him how to play baseball. He thought to himself, *I could still make her a great centerfielder.*

Betty Ann looked down at Jacelyn and with tears in her eyes said, "I can't wait to show you how to make Toll House cookies." Everyone laughed.

When Marie placed Jace in her father's arms, her little bundle of joy smiled up at her new grandparents. Marie gushed out happy tears. Her mom looked over at her daughter as tears streamed down her own face.

Within Betty Ann's family, they called this being "Uncle John," a reference to Betty Ann's brother John who cried at all family events. Even Donato, who always displayed a gruff exterior, though inside he was more like a teddy bear, was sniffling as his eyes watered up. When he looked down at Jacelyn, she looked back up at him smiling.

Of course, Anthony was next in line presenting their new daughter to his parents, Carol and Philip. It was the first time Marie had ever seen Anthony cry like that. She smiled at him as he looked over at her wiping his eyes. Tony's mom and dad couldn't be prouder.

His father said to him, "Now son, you've become a father and with that comes an incredible responsibility." Philip group hugged Marie, Tony, and Jacelyn.

Then it was Marie's turn again. She turned to her little Ida. They just looked at each other. Noni had her big Ida nonstop smile on her face. Marie's eyes welled up and happy tears continued streaming down her face. When she placed Jacelyn into the arms of her little Ida, Marie felt this incredible overwhelming warmth, something spiritual, almost like an electric jolt hit her, she couldn't describe it or understand it...but she felt it. Something that was intangible, yet as powerful as a crashing ocean wave.

As soon as Noni held her, Jace looked up at her Great-Grandmother Noni, laughed, and gurgled. Noni looked over at her granddaughter and said, "Jacelyn is truly a miracle...I told you before, she is a gift from God." And then she added, "Her coming into this family will be a blessing, a sort of a link to the past...I can just feel it. Look for the signs."

Then Jacelyn made the rounds with all the other relatives and friends. The rest of the day was just a happy family and a new baby celebration. Food, wine, prosecco, Sambuca shots, beer, desserts, laughter, and love.

+ + +

That night Tony and Marie were getting ready for bed. They were exhausted from the long and emotional afternoon. However, they were still on cloud nine, reliving the events of the day while looking at the Polaroid photos her Uncle Stan had taken.

They couldn't believe how blessed they were to have this little angel. They both stood over Jacelyn's crib and embraced in a loving hug. Marie's head resting on Anthony's left shoulder. Then they turned to each other and began lightly jumping up and down, silently high-fiving each other and mouthing..."Oh my God, we're now parents."

They began to snicker hysterically and had to quickly exit the bedroom so they wouldn't wake the baby. As they leaned against her bedroom door listening for sounds, they embraced and shared "I love yous" with each other.

Tony said, "I'm the world's luckiest guy." He then walked to the bathroom to get ready for bed.

As Anthony finished brushing his teeth, Marie heard him cough a few times.

"Are you OK?" She asked.

"Yeah," Anthony replied, "I just have this little tickle in my throat. I think the cold ocean air over the last few mornings hauling in our catch, may have caused it."

When Anthony got into bed, Marie looked over at him. "Just make sure you don't have a cold; you could give it to your daughter."

"I won't Bella."

Then Marie laughed and blurted out, "Oh my God, you, Anthony Joseph have a baby daughter."

They both chuckled like highschoolers, hugged, kissed goodnight, and fell asleep in each other's arms.

+++

Marie and Anthony were so blessed to have their parents and her little Ida nearby. Anthony called them their built-in babysitters.

It was now 1993 and Jacelyn was now two-and-a-half years old. Marie went back to her childhood home on Olmstead Terrace to visit her Noni. They kept up with their weekly coffee get-togethers, either at Marie's or her parents' house. She loved her childhood home and was always happy to see her mom, dad, and of course her Ida.

Her brother Mickey, after college, had moved closer to Portland, Maine for a job, while he played semi-pro baseball for the Boston Red Sox AA Team. All three of them were taking turns hugging, kissing, and making baby sounds with Jacelyn. Jace kept looking over to her mother, as if to say, *Who are all these strange human people?* Marie just looked on with a big, happy smile on her face.

Since it was a nice late summer afternoon, they were going to put Jace in her stroller for their walk. Noni walked out of the living room where Marie was feeding Jacelyn and went into her bedroom. She came back a few minutes later with an envelope with a few old black-and-white photographs.

"Marie my dear, ever since Jacelyn was six months old, something about this little girl has just made my mind wander. It wasn't until the other day I realized what it was." She pulled out a photo; it looked quite old and frayed.

Noni handed Marie the photo to look at. It showed two young girls smiling for the camera in a backyard with a large field in the background, shady trees on both sides and a two-story farmhouse.

Before Marie could ask who they were, Noni said, "This is a picture of my Aunt Generosa and my mother, Argia. It was taken in the backyard of my grandparent's house in Sant'Agostino. They were teenagers. Does anything look familiar?"

Marie scanned the photograph, her eyes sweeping back and forth between the two young girls. She looked up at Noni with confusion on her face.

Noni said, "Look closer at my Aunt Generosa."

It took Marie a minute or two, but then all of a sudden, a light bulb went off. Marie snapped her head up and looked over at Jace, then back to the photograph and then at her grandmother in astonishment and let out, "Oh my! Jacelyn looks just like her."

Noni smiled, "Your little angel is a connection to the past."

+++

They strapped Jace into the back seat of the car, along with her stroller and headed toward the waterfront. They pulled into the parking lot of McGarth's Restaurant, a local favorite place to eat. As Marie was unfolding the stroller for their weekly walk, Marie couldn't get out of her mind what Noni had said, *Your little angel is a connection to the past.*

They began their walk by strolling along the town pier toward the historic waterfront, passing Souza's Seafood on their right and Woods Seafood on their left. Friends of Marie would yell from their cars, "Hey sistas!"

Noni would just chuckle and wave hello. They were inseparable. They did seem more like sisters than grandmother and granddaughter.

As they walked around, to their left were the outer harbor views of Duxbury Beach, Saquish Beach, Clark's Island, and Plymouth Long Beach. As they made their way south, they passed the inner harbor, where Marie pointed to the boats and said, "Jace that's where Daddy works."

A large flock of seagulls (*gabbiani*) flew overhead and dove into the harbor as some fishermen were emptying their bait fish and fish guts from the days catch. As they continued, the Mayflower ship was tied up to the adjacent wharf and then the Portico displaying Plymouth Rock; though the locals affectionately called it "Our Pebble."

Several more people drove by tooting their horns, waved, and shouted out to Marie and Noni. Three generations of women walking along the historical waterfront. They'd wave back and then try to guess who it was. They got such a kick out of doing that. They stopped at Pebbles Restaurant across from the Mayflower and got two cups of coffee to go.

The sun was shining bright that day, so bright you had to shield your eyes from the glare bouncing off the water. They found a bench in Pilgrim Memorial Park and sat to enjoy the beautiful view of the harbor and Long Beach. Marie took Jacelyn out of her stroller and let her stumble her way onto the grass with her stuffed puppy dog Herbie.

After seeing the picture of Generosa, Marie asked Noni about her, "Ida, I know you've mentioned your Aunt Generosa before, but I don't remember her whole story. Wasn't she the one whose boyfriend died at a young age?"

Noni nervously fiddled with her hands and fingers and sadly looked up at Marie as a warm south ocean breeze came rolling through, as if the breeze was blowing back a painful memory.

"Yes, from what my mother shared over the years and from writing back and forth with my Aunt Generosa, Caesar was the love of her life. They had met when they were just kids as they lived in nearby towns. His father, Giuliano, would carry their farm produce by horse-drawn wagon, to the market in Renazzo with Caesar. Giuliano would stop by the home of his childhood friend, Luciano Trocchi, who was my great, great-uncle," Noni said. "In fact, your grandfather's father was a cousin to Giuliano."

She continued, "It wasn't until they became teenagers that Generosa would confide in my mother, how much she liked Caesar, and that someday she hoped to marry him. That's all she talked about, Caesar this, Caesar that." Noni paused and with sadness in her eyes looked out over the waterscape where Gurnet Lighthouse sat at the harbor's entrance.

"So, what happened?" inquired Marie.

Noni looked up with a sad expression and continued, "Well, the two eventually became inseparable and any chance Caesar got to go to her house or near her house, he would jump at the chance. When Generosa's father would go to Giuliano Buttieri's house to exchange tools or swap some food or supplies, Generosa was always on the horse-drawn wagon hoping Caesar was home.

"Both fathers would just laugh. Luciano was heard to say to Giuliano, 'We may be in-laws someday.' They both got a hardy chuckle out of it."

"Then what, my little Ida?"

"Well war broke out between Italy and Austria. It was a senseless war like most. It was silly, losing life over small chunks of land," she continued. "The local and surrounding rural areas never trusted their patchwork, corrupt government much. From what my mother and papa told me of the old days, I don't blame them."

Marie, Ida, and Jacelyn sat in the park enjoying the smell of the ocean and the sunny warm day. Marie gave Jace her bottle to keep her occupied. Marie reflected on what her grandmother had told her so far about Generosa and Caesar.

As if Noni could read Marie's mind, she said, "There's more to tell. How about we wait till you take me back to your parents' house, and I will make us some lunch?"

A few of Marie's friends stopped by the bench to say hi to her and Noni, and for a chance to meet Jace.

+++

After they returned to Marie's parents' house, she fed Jace again and put her down for a nap. As Marie looked down at the sleeping Jace, her mind kept going back to what her Ida had said earlier…"Your little angel is a connection to the past." *Wow…I wonder what Noni meant by that?*

Noni made a little lunch for them, Putung sandwiches from the old country. This was Marie's favorite sandwich. Putung (slang) consists of combining hamburger, Italian breadcrumbs, egg, salt, pepper, parmesan cheese, and a little nutmeg into a large oval patty about six inches long and three inches wide and then slowly frying it in an iron skillet with diced onions. Flipping it over and over till it is crispy brown on the outside, moist on the inside with the onions caramelized. After letting it cool, you cut it into slices, lay it on fresh bread, garnished with either mustard or ketchup. Marie preferred mustard. Sometimes Noni would pour fresh tomato sauce over the putung and add some peas to it for a dinner with fresh Italian bread.

As they settled in at the table, Marie couldn't wait to have Noni continue her story. She asked Noni if she had more pictures of Generosa and her family from the old country. It had been a while since Marie had seen any of these old photos.

"Yes, I do dear." Noni got up from her chair and went to her bedroom and into her dresser. She emerged with a shoebox and an old scrapbook with so many black and white photographs they were falling out of the book's sleeves and onto the floor as she walked back to the kitchen table.

Marie followed, picking up the scattered photos. Marie was just amazed how she had two families, one in Plymouth and one across the ocean in Italy. *How lucky am I?* she thought.

While they ate their sandwiches, Noni showed Marie a few more pictures of Generosa, her mother Argia, and other cousins from Italy. For each photograph, Noni tried to recall as much as she could remember from her mother's stories.

"So, my dear, Caesar and Generosa began to un-officially court, which was tradition, and they had to bring a chaperone with them when they went out. My mother actually chaperoned a few times."

Noni then giggled, "My mother told me she would look the other way whenever Generosa gave Caesar a little goodbye kiss on the cheek."

"Oh, how romantic," sighed Marie.

"Yes, it was very romantic. Then something trag-ic happened."...Noni looked down at her hands in deep thought and blessed herself.

"As I mentioned, a war had broken out. One morning, Caesar, who was up early to do his morning chores, had just sat down to eat the breakfast his mother had prepared. All of a sudden, a loud banging on the door disrupted their quiet morning."

Noni continued, "A group of military soldiers burst in and after exchanging some words with Giuli-ano and Teresa, claimed they had the right to con-script young men for the war effort against Austria."

Marie looked at her Ida in disbelief. "As my ma-ma tells the story, Caesar put up a fight, and he was knocked out cold by the butt of a rifle. When his father tried to step in, the soldiers pointed their guns at him. They carried the limp body of Caesar out the door and threw him into the back of a military truck...his fami-ly never heard from him again. Caesar's father searched all over for his son, even visiting the local police station on a weekly basis, but there was no word."

Marie looked at Noni in horror and tears began to trickle down her face. For an instant, she thought what if instead of Generosa and Caesar, it had been her and Anthony, and it made her cry even harder. Noni reached over and caressed her granddaughter's hand. Rubbing her fingers with hers. It was calming. Marie's heart and soul went out to her great-aunt, whom she had never met. Marie just ached, knowing what it would be like if she ever lost Anthony. In that moment, a warm flushing feeling went through Marie. She felt her body tingle. She felt an instant connection, a spiritual pang in her heart for her Great-Aunt Generosa.

Noni continued, "It wouldn't be until near the end of the war, that other young men taken that same day from the Cento area, returned home from the war and brought Caesar home in a coffin. He had died valiantly as the story goes.

"Generosa had never given up hope that Caesar would return to his family and her. She was seventeen then, and even though her parents insisted she move on with her life, find a nice man, get married, and have children, Generosa just couldn't.

"They would bury Caesar in the family cemetery. From what my mother told me, Generosa had asked Giuliano and Teresa that when she died if they would allow her to be buried next to him. They gave their permission."

+ + +

"So, whatever happened to Aunty Generosa?" asked Marie.

Noni fidgeted a little. "As I mentioned, she never gave up hope that Caesar would return. She eventually took over Novella's café where she had worked in her hometown of Renazzo, so she could keep herself busy and make a living. She was a hard worker, that one. She changed the name and called it Caffè dell'Amore Perduto...Lost Love Café, which she ran for over fifty years.

"In fact, Angelo Maini, my great-uncle, upon his retirement from his own café, gave her his large espresso machine as a gift, which she cherished. Even though it brought back sad memories of that day when she and Caesar had their picture taken, in a strange way it brought her closer to him. She buried herself in her café, making others happy while she silently suffered from heartbreak."

Marie just looked at her Ida as tears rolled down her face. She once again replaced Generosa and Caesar with her and Anthony...what would she do if she ever lost Anthony. Marie got up and went over to hug her little Ida.

17

A World Is Shattered (1995)

Marie had just turned thirty and had been married for ten wonderful years, and Jacelyn had just turned four. Anthony still had his nagging cough. He had gone to the doctors, on Marie's request, however, they couldn't find anything to pinpoint the source of the coughing. The doctor told him he needed to stop smoking.

After about two months, the cough got worse. He insisted it was just from being out on the ocean in the cooler weather as it was turning from fall to winter. Very soon he would be putting his lobster pots to rest and join his dad for only occasional winter fishing ventures.

After a few more weeks passed, Marie finally put her foot down and demanded he get an appointment to see a specialist at the Jordan Hospital. In fact, she was so worried, she called Dr. Angely directly to make the appointment.

"Anthony, you can't take these things lightly." Marie mused: *Those men, thinking they're so invincible. Men can be such bad patients. They think they are immortal and if they're sick...well they can't tell anyone, hurts their egos.*

Marie now wishes Anthony wasn't so macho. She wishes she had pushed him a little harder, been more persistent.

A few weeks later, the tests came back. Anthony had advanced lung cancer and was given eight to ten months to live. Their idyllic world just turned upside down in an instant.

Neither of them could feel a thing. The numbness flowed everywhere, through every inch of their bodies. They couldn't understand, *Why them? What had they done to deserve this?* Anthony did smoke, but only while he was at sea. Not a lot, but he always downplayed how much when Marie asked. She told him to stop for Jacelyn. He was trying, but he still snuck a few cigarettes while out on the boat. If she had known, she would have let him have it!

+ + +

Now came the hard part. They called both sides of the family to come over to the house. Before this gathering occurred, Marie had asked Cousin Paula if she could take Jace for the afternoon so as not to overwhelm and confuse her. Paula was glad to help. When everyone was assembled, Tony walked into the middle of the living room, with Marie at his side, holding hands and told everyone the news. The only sounds were gasps, sniffles, and tears. Everyone was devastated. Only Anthony seemed to be at peace with what was going on. He was always the rock for Marie, and now Jacelyn. Everyone joined Anthony in the middle of the room for a group hug and they all began to cry. After the group hug broke up, Anthony stepped back and took a knee, everyone followed his lead.

Father Santi from St. Mary's Parish in North Plymouth, walked into the middle of the group and led them in prayer. "Dear Lord and Savior, though sometimes we do not understand why events happen the way they do, we trust in your love and guidance. I know our faith in you is as strong as it has ever been, and I know you will look over this beloved family during their time of need. Dear Lord, we pray for you to put Your Healing Hands on Anthony and his lungs and ask in your infinite power to rid him of this disease. In our time of need, Lord, we ask you to Heal our brother Anthony. Amen."

Everyone again joined in a group embrace. Tony asked them all to please keep an eye on his family.

Later that afternoon, after everyone left, Paula dropped off Jacelyn. Marie and Anthony took little Jace aside and tried to explain to her that daddy was very sick and that they needed everyone to pray for him.

Without being instructed Jacelyn grabbed the hands of both her parents and said a little prayer, "Baby Jesus, please watch over my daddy and make him better Amen."

The two of them looked down at her with adoration and love. "That's my girl," Anthony said through tears.

+ + +

Over the next few months, Tony would still go off to work, though Marie wished he would stay home and rest, but he told her, "Mia Bella, at sea, the fresh salty air makes me feel alive and helps me keep my mind focused on taking care of my boat and the guys. I feel free being out on the water, free to think of you and Jace and pray to Jesus to cure me. I'll only work three days a week," he assured her, "and the guys have already agreed to take up my shift times. Hammy, (referring to his childhood friend, Jeff Hammond), will captain the boat the days I am not there."

Family and friends stopped by when he was home to sit with the two of them and reminisce about the old days.

After about four months, Tony became more tired and run down from the cancer treatments. The cancer continued to spread throughout his lungs. He kept a portable oxygen tank with him on the boat and at the house to help him recover from over exertion. It was a "pain in the ass," as he said, but it did help him breath a lot more easily.

On the days Anthony worked, Marie and Jacelyn would walk from their home and meet him down at the wharf. Jace would climb up on his shoulders as they made their way back home. Anthony looked at Marie, then Jace, and whispered, "I'm going to miss this."

Marie, with her arm around his waist, pulled him in for a big hug. They walked home in silence.

+++

It seemed they didn't even have enough time for Marie and Anthony to say their goodbyes. They would stand in their little kitchen having their homemade cappuccinos and just stare out at the backyard...the birds chirping away, playing nature's music like that of a well-seasoned choir while the grey squirrels chasing each other up and down the trees and through the limbs played a game of catch the leader. Why should they appear to have no worries at all, while her husband was dying of cancer?

Since they had told Jacelyn of her daddy's illness, she would also ask if he was OK, "Is Daddy feeling better today? Did my prayers work?"

"Yes baby, your prayers are making Daddy feel better. But he is still sick and has to stay home more, just like when you are sick and you stay home."

Within a month, Tony had stopped working altogether. He was just too tired and weak. He spent most of the time on the couch in their living room or on their back patio soaking in the warmth of the sun. His cough became constant as the cancer spread. Most days Jacelyn would cuddle with him on the couch or the outdoor patio, as he read some of her favorite books to her.

Every time he finished a book, she would look up at him and say, "Thank you Daddy...I love you."

There were times when Anthony broke down crying. Jace squeezed his hand and asked, "Why are you sad, Daddy, is it because you are not feeling good?"

Marie, upon hearing this, would appear and asked Jacelyn to help her in the kitchen. Anthony mouthed, "Thank you," to Marie with tears in his eyes.

There were other times when Jacelyn would fall asleep on the chest of her daddy with her arms around his neck. Anthony cherished those moments. While she slept, he would whisper in her ear that she was a big girl now and when daddy was gone, she was to take care of her mother.

Marie put a call out to all their family and close friends; Anthony would be staying home full-time. His buddies and boat crew would come by weekly to sit and reminisce about high school and what their friendships meant. Both Tony's and Marie's mothers were permanent fixtures at the house, helping out with cleaning, cooking, and taking Jace out for walks so Tony and Marie could be alone.

They decided a nurse should come in daily to keep Anthony comfortable and to help manage his pain. Luckily, Marie's cousin Paula was a nurse, and said that she'd love to help out. Paula would stop by at the end of the day from her shift at the Jordan Hospital. Paula even brought a small nurses cap and a toy stethoscope for Jace so she could help take her dad's blood pressure and listen to his heart.

Tony would chuckle and ask, "Are you going to grow up and be a nurse like Cousin Paula?"

Jace would look at her father, with the crooked nurse's cap on her little head and say, "You bet, Daddy! I'm gonna be a great nurse...right, Cousin Paula?"

"You betcha sista," Paula said with a big grin.

+++

That night Marie sat next to Anthony as he lay in bed. He took her hand and said, "I'm not going to get better, my love. I know ever one keeps saying 'get better,' but I know I'm not."

Marie laid her head gently on his chest. She just wanted to take in his smell and the beating of his heart. She felt safe here, as tears flowed out soaking into Anthony's T-shirt.

"Hey, you're getting me wet!" he chuckled. Marie sat up and wiped away the tears so she could look at him clearly. He then told her he would be keeping an eye on her and Jace. "Mia Bella, I just want you two to be happy."

"Follow your dreams, and if it means falling in love with someone else, I'm OK with that." Anthony also told her, "Follow your heart, it's the best compass of all, Bella."

He was giving her permission to move on.

Two weeks later, on July 13, 1996, Anthony passed away peacefully in their home surrounded by family and friends. Everyone there held hands, and

Father Santi led them in prayer. Marie and Jacelyn sat on the bed still holding Anthony's hand, weeping. Marie was devastated. She lost her best friend, her rock. As her parents stood behind her, they placed their loving hands on her heaving shoulders.

Four-year-old Jace had no idea what was happening. She just knew that Daddy was really sick, until Mommy told her, "Daddy has gone to live with Jesus and his angels."

"Mommy," she asked, "can we go and visit him, to make sure he is OK and happy?"

"We will someday baby," she told Jace. "We will someday."

+++

After the wake and funeral had come and gone, Marie just stayed in for a week, with Jacelyn and the immediate family. She had no energy to go out, and God forbid if she ran into someone she knew. She wasn't ready to handle it emotionally.

There were no words to describe how everyone felt, especially Marie, who caught herself staring off into space. Her mind wondering...wandering. Following that week, friends and other relations came to visit or to just "check-in" on her.

Everyone brought a meal to reheat or freeze, and the endless desserts were compliments of Mr. Borsari and his bakery. She didn't realize how small her little house was. Her cozy cape-style two-story home now felt like it was bursting at the seams. Most times, though, just a small group of family and close friends would come to sit and keep her company.

Sometimes it was so quiet you could hear the ticking of their General Electric circular, porcelain wall clock with pink roses at the twelve, three, six, and nine marks. Its regimented tick, tick, tick, counting away physical time, like the sand at the ocean's edge that chases the water back into the ocean, forever. Not many words were exchanged. You could feel the loneliness in her house. Her only saving grace was Jacelyn.

Over the next few months, aside from the tears and the heartache, she wondered what she would do now. She'd known only one man her entire life. Her rock! Though Marie was tough as nails, she felt helpless, numb, almost zombie-like at times. *What will I do?* she kept repeating to herself. She heard Anthony's voice in her head, *Follow your dreams Bella.*

The next day Noni mailed a letter to Generosa telling her of Anthony's passing.

+ + +

Several months after Anthony's funeral, Marie, with the blessing of her parents, asked her little Ida, "I'm wondering if you could see your way to moving in with Jace and me. I could really use your help, and your company. This house feels so empty."

Noni didn't even hesitate. "Yes, my dear...I was actually going to ask you if I could." They hugged...then cried a little. A big weight had been lifted from Marie's shoulders.

She looked up to Heaven and said, "Thank you, my love."

18

Marie's Dream

About six months later, Marie realized her savings and the life insurance policy from Anthony's passing wouldn't last forever. She needed to get out and start making a new life for Jace and herself. Not that she wanted to move on into a relationship; that was the furthest thing from her mind. She just needed to find some normalcy, a regular routine, the stability she once had up until Anthony's passing.

Noni offered to help out financially. She gave what she could, though she proved most valuable as a great built-in babysitter to Jacelyn and a mental support system for Marie.

Still Marie kept asking herself, *What can I do?* She could hear Anthony's voice saying, *Follow your dreams, Mia Bella.*

She still worked at Borsari's Bakery on Court Street in North Plymouth where she had been working since high school. Mr. Borsari told her to come back to work when she felt up to it. But could she? It would be like stepping back into her old life. All those memories of Anthony sitting on his favorite stool at the counter by the front window, a worn-out, padded red vinyl top, spinnable stool waiting for Marie to get off work. Should she do that or "paint on a new canvas?"

Marie thought out loud to herself, *Was it time for me to follow my dream? I had confided in Anthony about it, before he passed away. Wow, is it time to open my own small café? Where would I begin?*

She prayed night and day that God and Anthony would help guide her to her new path; her new life for her and Jace. She felt lost, alone, and afraid.

+++

One night there was a huge thunderstorm with crackling lightning that shook her house. From her top floor bedroom, she could see the storm rolling off a turbulent sea causing havoc for the boats moored on the inner jetty of the harbor. As the thunder cracked and boomed, bolts of lightning crashed to the ground, illuminating her room.

Suddenly she could hear the frantic footsteps of her little one racing down the hallway, her feet thumping in chorus with the storm outside. Jace opened Marie's bedroom door and leapt from the doorway to her mom's bed without hitting the floor.

"Mommy, Mommy, I'm scared!" Jace frantically yelped.

Marie hugged and comforted her daughter with a reassuring smile on her face. "Now what did I tell you about thunder, Jace?"

"You told me that it's just the angels bowling in Heaven," Jacelyn whispered, still frightened by the loud sounds. An old wives tale that Marie's mom used to say to her when she was little...and it worked!

Jace eventually fell asleep in her arms. Marie couldn't feel more blessed to have this little angel in her life. She thought, *You are a special little girl.* Marie closed her eyes and followed Jacelyn into dreamland.

+++

About an hour later, right before another big bolt of lightning hit, Marie had a dream, one of her recurring dreams since Anthony died.

In the dream, Anthony would be at the water's edge, small wakes of water splashing over his bare feet. The sand retreating over and under his toes, sinking his feet deeper into the wet sand. He is holding out his arms to her. She'd run to him, however each time before she made it to the waterline, Anthony would fade from sight. She would be left standing there on the beach all by herself, arms raised. She'd always wake up to a wet pillowcase, feeling depressed, hopeless, and so missing her rock.

But this time, her dream was different, it felt different. As she made her way to the water's edge, Anthony was there and took ahold of her hands. She could feel the roughness of his hands, smell him, she could feel his presence, his spiritual force. She hugged him, and it felt like it had always been. As they looked into each other's eyes, it no longer felt like a dream. It felt like...for this moment...they were reunited, physically together. Tears rolled down her face as she looked up into Anthony's eyes.

He looked down at her and said, "Mia Bella...I know you and Jacelyn are in pain. It breaks my heart, but life can be a difficult journey, and things happen for a reason. Please keep your heart open to hear God's voice and look for the signs, just like Noni always says."

"Are you OK Anthony?"

"Mia Bella, I am wonderful, I've been reunited with so many family and friends here...it is truly Heaven, and I am also out of pain my love, I am now free to keep an eye on you and Jace."

"But..." Marie couldn't finish her words.

"I miss and love you so very much, Marie."

As she continued looking up at him with teary eyes. He explained to her, "I've been watching you ever since I passed, and felt I needed to 'visit' you. I know you are at a crossroads of figuring out what you are supposed to do with your new, unexpected life. Follow your dreams Mia Bella...follow your dreams, follow your instincts, follow your heart...." Anthony kept repeating this until he faded from her embrace.

As she came out of her dream, she felt the wetness on her pillow from her tears. However, this time she didn't feel the hopelessness or despair of the past. She felt an enormous rush of warmth and pure love that seemed to flow through her and embrace her entire body, like the first sip of hot cocoa on a cold winter's day. The lightning struck one more time as if Anthony was announcing his departure.

Suddenly Jace rolled over toward Marie, opened her eyes and said groggily, "Daddy told me to tell you he loves you very much."

Jace then rolled back over and went back to sleep. Marie knew right then and there, it wasn't a dream, Anthony had come to visit her, to assure her whatever she chose to do was the right path. She made her decision. Marie could only cry tears of gratitude as she fell asleep with her little angel in her arms.

+++

When she awoke that morning, she came down from her bedroom into the kitchen; Noni had already made Jacelyn her favorite breakfast: waffles, fresh blueberries, syrup, and a large glass of milk. She was already halfway through her first waffle.

"Good morning, my dear," Noni said. "Quite the storm last night, did you sleep OK?"

Marie recalled the crazy thunder and lightning storm in the middle of the night and wondered about everything she had experienced and what it all meant. All she knew was she felt refreshed, anew; she felt purposeful and compelled to follow her dream. "Yes, I did Ida, the first good night sleep I've had in a while."

Noni raised an eyebrow and gave her a slight nod and a smile. Noni washed the dishes and then went into the living room to dust. Her favorite house chore.

Marie leaned over Jace and kissed her on the forehead. Then said, "Jace, does Daddy come to you in your dreams?"

Jace had just turned five years old and it took Jace a minute for the question to register in her mind. She sheepishly looked at her mommy and said, "Yes, I dream about Daddy a lot. He tells me what a special girl I am. He says I'm Mommy's big girl, and I'm supposed to take care of you."

Marie's eyes welled up, then her tears overflowed, like a small puddle constantly fed water from a roof run-off. She placed her hand over her gaping mouth to hide her surprise. Then she leaned over and hugged her little girl. "Jace honey, why haven't you told me before that Daddy comes to you in your dreams?"

"I don't know, Mommy," Jace said, looking up with her big brown eyes. "I hear you cry at night, and I know you miss Daddy. I don't want to make you sad."

Marie stood there biting her lower lip as it quivered. "Jace, you wouldn't make me sad; I would be happy if you told me. Promise Mommy next time Daddy comes to you in a dream, you'll tell me. You will make Mommy very, very happy."

"OK Mommy I will," she said. Looking up into her mother's eyes, then like a shy puppy dog added, "Daddy always says he loves you very much, too."

Finishing the last gulp of milk and bite of her waffle, Jace got up from the table and went into the living room to play. Marie refilled her coffee cup and sat down at the kitchen table, tears still streaming down both cheeks. She looked around the kitchen, reliving so many wonderful memories that came flooding back to her, like the slow leak of a dam before it collapses. She buried her head into her folded arms on the kitchen table and sighed. "Anthony, thank you for visiting me last night. I feel so much better knowing you are OK and out of pain. I miss you so much. I so need your help and guidance, and please come visit me soon you lughead!" she said with a smirk.

After a few minutes of grieving, she picked up her head, wiped the tears from her eyes, and knew it was time to act.

19

The Café Is Born

Marie took out a notebook and began to lay out her plan. Her high school history teacher, Mrs. Estes, came to mind. She once demonstrated how the students could use a "focus wheel" technique to help in writing their upcoming term papers on the Battle of Lexington and Concord in April of 1775.

Marie sat down at the kitchen table, opened the notebook and drew a big wheel in the middle of the page; then she added spokes coming off the wheel, like an eight-legged spider. Under the main spokes were smaller lines. In the middle of the circle, like a bullseye, she wrote the word "CAFÉ." At each spoke she jotted down a category or item she would need; like possible locations, how big her café needed to be, what items to sell in her café, what types of equipment, and permits. She would double check with Mr. Borsari to help her with the look and feel of her café as well as taking a look at her business plan. She would have to tell him soon about her plans.

Of course, a name for her café. She thought to herself...*wow a name...that is going to be hard.* She wrote down several names. One was Marie's Café, but she felt funny naming her café after herself. She thought of Angel's Café, as her little daughter was her angel. *That Jace,* she thought...a gleam came to her eye...as if being prompted by an invisible hand. Marie reached over, picked up the pen and finally wrote down JACE'S—the one thing that connected her and Anthony.

"That's it, Jace's Café!" she yelled. She couldn't wait to tell her parents. Just then Noni walked back into the kitchen. "Noni, I have a name for my café... Jace's Café."

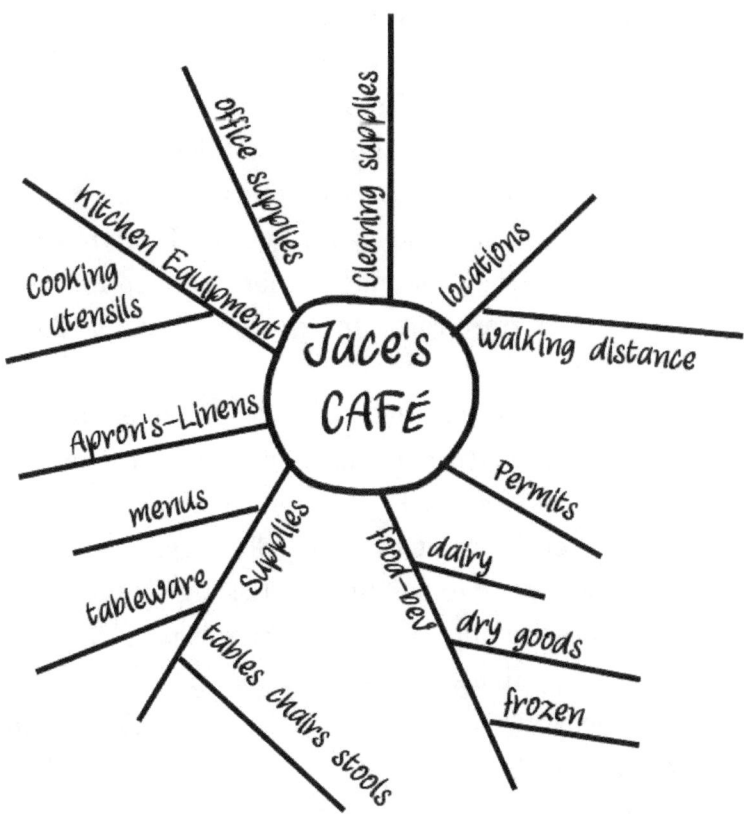

Noni smiled and said, "I was hoping that would be the name. As I told you, she is a connection to the past...now that includes our beloved Anthony. Remember, follow the signs."

+++

She knew pretty much everyone in Plymouth and the surrounding towns from growing up there and working at the local bakery. She wanted to stay near her family, so maybe downtown Plymouth would be a great spot. The historical downtown area was so quaint, with Burial Hill, Town Square, views of Plymouth Harbor, and First Street [known today as Leyden Street]. This is where the original location of the Plimoth Plantation stood. Being close by her family, they would be able to keep an eye on Jacelyn when Marie was working. She made a note to keep her eyes open for some storefronts to rent on Main or Court Streets.

Marie was so excited about everything and she remembered how Anthony had orchestrated the construction to make their house more livable. Could she do this without Anthony's help? She began to panic, but the next moment she felt him looking down on her. She remembered then, before Anthony passed away, he told her, "I will always be there for you."

She looked to Heaven and said, "Well, Anthony...here we go!"

Her list included a large industrial coffee maker, a large refrigerator with adjoining freezer, a baking oven, a license from the town, which included a certificate from the health department. Hmmm, what about also serving espresso and cappuccino? She loved the espresso and cappuccino's she made at home and nobody else was offering it. She also recalled Noni saying, "Generosa served *the best* espresso and cappuccino at her café in Renazzo."

So, in honor of her Great-Aunt Generosa, she would add these to the menu.

The next day she grabbed Jace and Noni and went to see Mr. Borsari at his bakery. She wanted to be the first to thank him for all of the experience he had given her at his bakery, and tell him about her new idea, her café.

He was so excited for her. Marie was the daughter he never had and always had a special place in his heart for her. He had also been great friends with her grandfather, Nino. Mr. Borsari was so broken up after Tony passed away, while he assured her she would always have a job at his bakery, he was even more excited that she was taking the leap to start her own business.

He led them over to an empty table and started to give her some ideas on what to include in her list for the café. The last item he wrote down on his list was "Love."

Marie looked inquisitively at him and said, "Love?"

Mr. Borsari chuckled and in his broken English said, "If a you don't put a love in your a baking or in a you life, it just doesn't taste as a good!" Marie just smiled.

"Have a you thought about a location?" Mr. Borsari asked.

"Well, I just decided yesterday morning, but I would like a place people could walk to and also have ample parking. A place I could walk to and near my family. Oh, I want to be far enough away so you know my café won't compete with your bakery!"

Mr. Borsari smiled, then said, "Of course. I have a real estate friend. Let a me ask him to keep an eye open for the perfect location."

+++

Marie was so happy that her Ida was now living with her. She was such a big help with Jace, and her presence filled in the lonely times when she missed Anthony.

Every night while Marie lay in bed she would talk to Anthony and ask him for a sign that she was doing the right thing.

One night she felt especially lonely, looked over at the empty space next to her, and began to cry. She hugged the pillow and got so mad at Anthony for dying. She knew it was selfish, but she had so many big life decisions to make by herself, and she felt like all the pressure was on her. She felt like she was chasing their dreams all by herself. In frustration, she began to cry harder than she had for some time.

A few minutes later there was a soft knock on her door. It was Noni. She would occasionally pop in to say goodnight before she went to bed. "Hi sweetie, are you OK? I heard you crying and just want to make sure there isn't something you need."

"Come on in my little Ida, you're the best. I'm just scared about taking this big step in opening up my own Café. What if I fail?"

Noni sat on the edge of the bed and rubbed the inside of Marie's forearm with her fingertips. Something she always did. Noni just looked at her and said, "What if you don't fail?"

Marie smiled as her eyes welled up. "Ida you always have an answer, don't you?"

Noni smirked and said, "Sometimes, but when I don't, I ask God to help me. I listen to His voice and watch for His signs. Always watch for the signs my dear. Now, get some sleep." With that, Noni got up, put Marie's arm back under the blanket, smiled, then walked out, and closed the door behind her.

Marie lay staring at the ceiling as she pulled her sheets under her chin...*Watch for the signs.*

+ + +

The next morning, Marie received a phone call.

"Hello, Mr. Borsari!"

"Marie, are you a busy now? Come see me at the courthouse, outside on the front sidewalk."

He didn't give her time to say no, and she could hear the excitement in his voice.

"Yes, I can be there in about fifteen minutes."

"Noni, that was Mr. Borsari on the phone. He's asked me to meet him downtown at the courthouse. I hope you can watch Jacelyn for me? I'm not sure for how long."

"Of course. That's what I am here for," replied Noni.

"Oh, thank you!" Marie got ready and then bolted out her door and briskly walked up Howland Street to Court Street. She crossed over Court Street, past the Coldwell Banker Building, and headed to the court-house on the west side of the street.

When she met up with Mr. Borsari he was stand-ing on the sidewalk next to a tall gentleman, wearing a business suit.

"Andrew Balboni, this is a Marie who wants you to find a good a place for her café.

"Marie, Andrew is local realtor. I ask a Andrew to help us find a location for you...so should a we go see these places?" He said in his broken English.

"Yes, yes please," begged Marie, clasping her fin-gers together.

As they walked south toward Shirley Square from the courthouse, they crossed the street and passed several storefronts. One of the owners of Pil-grim Progress, stepped outside to say hi and to pay her respects to Marie on the loss of Anthony. After a strong embrace, Marie told her she was going to open up a café in the area.

"That is such great news, Marie. I will be a regu-lar." said Mrs. Brigida.

Marie took that as a good sign!

As they continued on their way, Andrew said, "The first place is just across North Street at Shirley Square. It's the old Standish Deli, which, as you know, the building has been in continuous operation with different owners for decades."

"I love this old building!" Marie exclaimed.

As Andrew opened the door, Marie walked in and with just one quick look around, like a kid eyeing a dessert showcase full of their favorite pastries, her eyes were as wide as silver dollars. As she walked in, it was like stepping into her dream...suddenly, the whole interior took form, her vision of what she had imagined was being created in front of her eyes.

This is exactly how she envisioned her café to look. The placement of the counters, the appliances, the dessert cases, the seats and tables, the walls painted in mauve and light blue, framed pictures up on the walls, the lighting fixtures, everything laid right out there. And a big front picture window facing Court and Main Street. Three smaller windows around the side on North Street. This would allow people to look in and see what was going on.

"Wow, this is incredible...I love it! And this is my dream location!" exclaimed Marie, jumping with excitement.

Andrew and Mr. Borsari guided Marie to the back of the space where the ovens would be, the bathroom, and the prepping area for food and pastries. Marie was speechless. Her eyes welled up. She thought out loud, "Anthony what do you think?"

Mr. Borsari walked over to her and put his arm around her and said, "He would be a so proud of a you, Marie."

Andrew interjected and said, "Should we go look at the other space?"

"No...no...this is it!" said Marie. "But how much is the rent?" She said through squinted eyes.

Andrew looked over at Mr. Borsari with a smile. Mr. Borsari turned to Marie and said, "I knew a you would love a this place, there is no need to a look elsewhere. As a my gift to you, I a had Andrew draw up a rental agreement for this a location."

Holding the papers up for her to see, "I have a paid your first a year's rent."

Marie almost collapsed onto the floor; she had to grab a hold of the counter to keep from falling over. "Oh my God, Oh my God, Mr. Borsari, you don't have to do that!"

She blessed herself then said, "I am at a loss for words." With that, Marie went over and hugged him and began to sob on his shoulder.

She then heard Noni's voice in her head...*Look for the signs.*

20

Sad News from The Old Country

Ida grew up in Plymouth in a household where her
mother and father spoke mostly broken English, so
her Italian had regressed quite a bit. Actually, as they
grew older, their mother, Argia, told them they all
needed to "become Americans," so she discouraged
them from speaking Italian in the household. Though
because their parent's didn't know much English, they
did speak some Italian at home. So, as they grew up
from young children to teenagers to young adults, they
lost most of their native tongue and written word.

She could write her letters to Generosa in rough
Italian, but the challenge was always getting letters
back from Italy translated into English. Finely, she
began sending her letters in English to Luca, Generosa's nephew, who would then read them aloud to her
as he translated the English into Italian. Then Generosa would respond back to Luca, who translated into
English and then mailed the letters back to Ida.

Luca was Gianni's son, Generosa's brother
(*figlio*). Generosa once confided to her mother, Argia,
that Luca was like a son to her. In fact, when Generosa retired a few years ago from her café Luca took
over for her.

One morning, a few months later, after the mail
carrier dropped off the mail, Ida noticed a letter from

Italy. She looked closer and saw it was from Luca. Generosa told Ida in the letter to give Marie and Jacelyn a hug and kiss and sympathies on Anthony's passing. Everyone in Italy was in good health and spirits. They send their love and prayers.

For years Ida had written back and forth about every six months to her family in Italy; mostly to Generosa in Renazzo and other family members in Sant'Agostino. Even though it had been decades since Ida visited Italy, she felt it was important to stay deeply connected with her family. Most letters were about the happenings going on with everyone's family both here in the US and Italy; stories about Jacelyn and a few new pictures of her. Ida also mentioned that Marie was planning to open her own café, just like her Great-Aunt Generosa.

+++

A month later, Marie padded into the kitchen to get some fresh coffee to start her day. Noni was sitting at the kitchen table with a letter dangling from her left hand and tears flowing down her face as her shoulders heaved up and down.

Marie raced right to her and wrapped her arms around her. "What's wrong, my little Ida?"

It took Noni a few minutes to compose herself. Then she looked up at Marie with red watery eyes. She had just received a letter from Luca saying Generosa had passed away, just a week ago. "He says, be-

156

fore my Aunt passed away, she wanted to make sure to tell you how much she loved you and your family and that she's never forgotten any of you."

Noni cried even harder. Marie held onto her as hard as she could without breaking her in two.

As Noni got her composure back, she added, "Luca was having to sell the café as he had a great opportunity to work with the Cento municipality. No one else in the family wanted to take over the day-to-day responsibilities of running a café."

She continued, "From my most recent letter to Generosa, he learned about you, Marie, opening your café in Plymouth, and one of Generosa's dying wishes was to ship the espresso machine she had in her café for over fifty years to you. The same espresso machine her Uncle Angelo gifted to her when she opened up her café so many years ago."

Even though the machine was not in working order, Generosa wanted to pass it down as a family heirloom and good luck charm.

Marie reached over to console her grandmother. "Signs, Noni...signs," said Marie, with a full closed-lip smile.

Luca added a side note: "We buried her next to Caesar and we knew Aunt Generosa was going straight to Heaven, when upon dying, a soft blue light covered her entire body. It was a calming and beautiful moment."

"Oh, my Ida I am so sorry, hunny. I know how close the two of you were."

Marie couldn't believe her ears. "Oh my. I can't believe she wanted me to have her espresso machine. Aunty Generosa's own espresso machine."

She heard Anthony in her mind say, *There is a reason for everything Mia Bella.*

She started to cry and gave Noni a big hug.

Noni looked at her granddaughter, smiled, and said, "Another God wink!"

21

The Café Takes Shape (1996)

Since taking over the space at Shirley Square, Marie went to her new café almost every day like clockwork. She was still working a few days a week at Borsari Bakery & Deli. Mr. Borsari was so happy for the daughter he never had, something he told her often. He knew she would be a success and was so proud of her.

After work at the bakery or her café, she'd hurry home, open the door and greet Jace who always ran to her in the hallway. After her big hug, Jace would grab her mother's hand and tell her all about her day. Marie knew Jace was a talker, so she'd smile as she kept Jace moving in a forward direction to find Noni in the kitchen. She'd then proceed to give Noni a big squeeze.

Frankly, between the café and raising Jace, that's what kept Marie going; kept her focused. She wanted to find her new purpose!

Within the first couple of weeks, she, along with her parents, her brother Mickey, the in-laws, cousins, and Tony's friends, who were mostly tradesmen or handy that way, designed and built-out the café.

Sometimes Jacelyn would accompany her mom at the café, but not this particular day. Jace was home with Noni so she wouldn't get in the way. Just as the build out was close to completion...an old tan Ford pick-up truck pulled up out front with a couple of older men Marie knew from Mr. Borsari's bakery. Without saying more than, "Compliments of Signore Borsari," they walked in the furniture they'd brought, piece by piece, and positioned tables and chairs along the left side wall...just where she had pictured it in one of her dreams.

She shook her head in disbelief, looked up to Heaven and said a prayer for Mr. Borsari.

That final day, with everyone gathered, including Jacelyn and Noni, they all stood back and admired their work. As Marie looked around the café, tears welled up in her eyes. They all took a few steps back and gave Marie her "moment."

She slowly looked around her café and saw the large chrome industrial refrigerator and freezer against the back left wall, like a pair of guardians keeping watch. Behind the faux wall to the right were the baking ovens. The dessert showcase was to the right as you walked in, where delectable desserts and pastries would eventually be displayed for purchase. The industrial coffee maker and the new espresso machine were stationed on a long, twelve-foot counter with a sink behind the dessert case. In the front of the café under the picture window, Marie placed a six-foot wooden oak table to fit Generosa's espresso machine when it arrived from Italy. Passers-by could then see the antique espresso machine through the window from Main Street. The checkout counter and register were just to the right as you walked in.

To the immediate left, under the first two windows overlooking North Street, was a ten-foot countertop, one of Tony's friends built for customers to sit at. In that same area, she placed the four 1970s style Formica topped circular tables with matching vinyl covered chairs, given to her by Mr. Borsari. Both tabletop and chairs were splashed with black and pink blotches. Her dream café.

It had been a long day, but they got so much accomplished. She thanked everyone and with Jace and Noni in tow they headed home for supper.

+ + +

It had been such a hardship losing Anthony. There were days when she wanted to just give up, throw in the towel, lay her head down, fall asleep in hopes of waking up from her life without Tony, and go back to the life she had before. Within seconds a kaleidoscope of happy memories came cascading back to her like an intermittent waterfall. Now it was all coming together. She knew she had to move forward. No giving up. *Follow your dreams, Mia Bella,* she heard Anthony say in her head. She knew Anthony would be proud of her.

As her eyes moved from left to right around the newly renovated café, she cupped her hands over her mouth and squealed with astonishment and wonder. Jacelyn walked over and grabbed her mother's hand, who was swaying right and left with her feet planted, taking it all in. Marie made the sign of the cross and knelt to say a blessing. Without hesitation, everyone else in the café followed suit. It was quite a sight to see.

Marie looked around at her friends, smiled, and began, "Dear Lord, thank you for answering my prayers, for filling me and everyone here with your Divine light and inspiration. I am so blessed to be in this family and with my incredible friends, and of course, our Jacelyn," as she tapped the top of Jace's head.

"Anthony, I know you're here right now...thank you for guiding me as well as reminding me to follow my dreams." There wasn't a dry eye in the café.

A few days later a big yellow and black delivery truck pulled up in front of the café. Two men walked in and said they were from Howie's Trucking and had a large, crated box for Marie.

With a big smile and a hop into the air, she proclaimed, "That's me!"

The two men climbed into the back of the truck, lowered the gate, and emerged with a wooden crate, about four-feet high by three-and-a-half-feet wide. Marie saw an import stamp on the side that said ITALY. She immediately went to grab the phone, hanging on the wall beside the cash register. As she picked it up and, in her haste, she got herself tangled up around the dark green phone cord and almost tripped herself.

She called home to Noni with so much enthusiasm she was talking a hundred miles an hour. She was finally able to say, "The espresso machine just arrived!" She couldn't hold back her inner child as the excitement burst through. "Can you and Jace come right down? I don't want to open it until you get here...hurry!"

"We're on our way!" Noni replied joyfully, accompanied by her Ida laugh.

+++

As the men wheeled the crate in, she directed them to its new home. "This is pretty heavy Ma'am; Where would you like us to put it?"

"Oh, on the big oak table over there under the picture window, please...but can you wait about ten minutes for my grandmother and daughter to get here and share in the moment?" she said in anticipation.

"Sure can," said one of the delivery guys.

Marie squealed, "That's great!" Then she added, "How about a fresh cup of coffee and homemade pie while we wait."

"It's a deal," said the second man, as he stepped forward, leaving the wooden crate on the floor for unpacking.

As Noni and Jace came hurrying through the front door, the bell chimed from above their heads. "Mommy, that sounds like the bell in that movie you like...that George guy with the angel wings. I like that movie, Mommy."

Jace ran over, lunged, and wrapped her little arms around her mommy as she gave her a big bear hug; and said, "Mommy that's a big present."

"It sure is sweetie."

After finishing their pie and thanking Marie profusely, the two men each grabbed a crowbar and started pulling out nails from the top side of the crate. Then the sides, which exposed the antique espresso machine. They began pulling away industrial stuffing and insulation and the folded cardboard that helped wedge the espresso machine in place during its long journey. It was still held in place by metal strapping, wrapped around the machine, a bunch of old towels wedged in for stability.

As they were lifting it off of the crate bottom, unseen by all, a small envelope slid under the dessert showcase.

Marie and Jacelyn were jumping up and down, as Noni looked on with a big smile.

"On top of this table Ma'am?" said one of the workers.

"Yes, please!" Marie said with girlish excitement.

They picked up the espresso machine and walked it carefully over to the large oak table under the picture window and gently placed it down.

"Perfect" Marie said. "Would you guys like another slice of pie?"

"Wow, Ma'am, that would be real kind of you!"

They all stood in front of the espresso machine, marveling at this precious gift from Generosa. It was made of shiny copper, stood about two-and-a-half-feet high and about two-feet wide. Even though the machine no longer worked, it would still be a prize possession of Jace's Café. Even now people walked by on the sidewalk and peered in, as the sun gleaned off the copper armor of the espresso machine.

Noni asked if they could all hold hands. Even the two delivery guys joined in. Noni started. "Dear Lord, thank you for all the blessings you have bestowed upon my wonderful family. I know that my Nino, Anthony, and Generosa will continue to watch over us and watch over my sweet Marie and her little angel as they follow their new dream...Amen."

In unison an echo went through the café... "Amen!"

22

Jacelyn's New Friend

A few days after Generosa's espresso machine arrived, Jace was at the front of the café, behind the
dessert display case. Marie was busy putting up some
beautiful color and black-and-white framed photos on
the walls in the bathroom and around the café. The
photos were of the historic Plymouth Waterfront, the
Mayflower, Plymouth Rock, and Town Square.

She also acquired an old, framed pencil sketch of
the Winslow House on Shirley Square, the original
building that her café now occupied. The sketch was
from 1757, when the house was then occupied by
James Warren and his wife Mercy Otis. He served as
the President of the Massachusetts Provincial Con-
gress and Paymaster General of the Continental Army. She was the sister of the famous Colonial Jurist,
James Otis of Barnstable, on Cape Cod. What a history to live up to!

As the music of the sixties, seventies, and eight-
ies played on the radio, compliments of WBCN, Marie
heard Jace having a conversation with someone. As
she listened to Jace's animated conversation, Marie
just smiled and went back to her work.

But after a few more minutes, Marie called out,
"Jace, who are you talking to?" Marie again smiled to
herself...maybe it's an imaginary friend, she thought,

with a chuckle. No response. Marie remembered herself as a little girl of five, having an imaginary friend who she played alongside with her Barbie doll. They would both take turns dressing Barbie in different outfits.

Jace just kept on talking and having a lively one-way conversation. After a little while, Jace came walking to the back of the café, near the storage closet, to the bathroom where her mom was.

"Jace, who were you talking to? Sounded like you were having quite the conversation."

Jace excitably looked up at her mom with her big brown eyes and exclaimed, "The old lady with the white hair. She's my new friend, Mommy!"

"That's great, hunny. What's her name?" asked her mom.

"Her name is Rose, and she is so nice, Mommy," Jacelyn replied.

Marie smiled as she touched Jacelyn's shoulders. "What does she look like?"

Jace looked up into the corner of her memory, trying to put it all together in her own words. "She is old, like Noni and has short grey and white hair, like Noni, with a big smile. She is so sweet."

"Where is she now?" Marie smiled.

Jacelyn pointed over to the antique espresso machine. "There by the funny coffee machine," as she called it. She had trouble pronouncing the word espresso.

Marie smiled. "How nice. What were the two of you talking about?"

With the innocence of a child, Jace looked up into her mommy's eyes and said, "She said she is excited you are opening your café...said you will do good."

Marie chuckled, "Well, I guess your new friend will be my first employee. Did she say anything else, Jace?"

Jacelyn bit her lower lip and sheepishly said, "She said she'd come back soon."

With an inquisitive expression, Marie looked at her little angel and said, "Well, I'm glad you have a new friend, but we need to finish up here and get home for dinner."

"OK, Mommy."

+ + +

As the days went by, the café began to take shape...like taking a chunk of soft clay, then shaping, molding, shaping again till it was near perfect. The vision she had when she first started dreaming of her café was coming to life before her eyes.

Many of her childhood friends and friends of her parents would stop by, poke their head in the door to see what was going on. Others, like tourists, were just curious about what new business was opening. Many people popped their heads in and commented on the antique espresso machine. Marie would have to then stop what she was doing and tell everyone who asked the story. She finally had her cousin Paula type up a little story on a large index card and place it next to the espresso machine for when she officially opened. She hoped this would do the trick.

The only annoyance was the little bell above the door that kept chiming every time someone entered the café. After about eight chimes in one hour, Marie rolled her eyes and with a smirk on her face, took the broom handle bottom and pushed upward against the bell's support arm clearing it of any contact with the door. "Now that's progress," she chuckled to herself.

Even Mr. Borsari stopped by carrying a half dozen framed photographs from the walls of his own bakery. They were of his hometown in Cento, Italy. He also instructed his nephew to carry in the brand new three-legged stools, with red vinyl seat cushions for the café's ten-foot countertop—six of them in all. Marie looked at him in astonishment. "Mr. Borsari, oh my goodness, you didn't have to do this!"

He just looked at her, cupped his hands around her face and smiled, "I've a told you before...you are like a the daughter I a never had; you make a me proud. With love from a Sofia and me."

She was so overwhelmed her eyes started welling up. All the emotions from Anthony's passing, the love she had for her little Jacelyn, and now the outpouring of love from Mr. Borsari and so many others was just too much for her to contain herself. He hugged her and said, "Remember Marie...you a follow your dreams."

She felt a jolt of electricity run through her. "That's what Anthony always told me," she said with a sad smile.

"So, when do you a open up a your café?" he inquired.

"I'm hoping in about less than two weeks. We'll open up without much fanfare two Wednesday's from now as a dry run before we officially open that Saturday. It seems so far away, Mr. Borsari, but I know it will be here soon."

"I will a be your first customer," he said proudly as he straightened out his white pressed dress shirt and brown tie.

23

Jacelyn's Friend Visits Again

With the café's opening about a week away from Wednesday, everyone, spearheaded by Marie and Noni, were in high gear. Her mom, brother Mickey, cousin Paula, and Marie's best friends, Ann and Elise, and of course Jace were all ready to go.

Everything was coming together. Some more dry goods were being delivered. Ten-pound bags of coffee beans, flour, sugar, paper goods, serving plates, coffee and espresso cups with saucers and large cappuccino cups, forks, knives, and spoons.

She proudly displayed her occupancy and health inspection permits on the wall next to the entrance along with the menu. Outside, by the doorway, Marie made sure the doggie bowl was full of fresh water.

+++

As people began to leave after finishing their duties, and hugs and kisses all around, Marie sat down at the table and just blew out a big sigh of relief as she wound down from another long day at the café. "I can't believe we made it this far," she whispered to herself.

Within a few minutes, she heard Jace carrying on another one-way conversation like last week in the back of the café. She was talking up a storm. Marie called from the front of the café, "Is your friend back?"

"Yes, Mommy. Rose says hi."

"Well, tell her I said hi back." Marie picked up some more paper goods and carried them to the supply closet at the back of the store, where Jacelyn was. She peeked around the corner at her daughter and as you can imagine, there she was, all three and a half feet of her, carrying on an animated conversation looking at the space in front of her. As Jace's conversation ended she turned and walked over to her mommy.

"She told me to tell you, she is looking forward to our café opening," Jace said with excitement in her voice.

"That's nice...we all are looking forward to opening as well," said Marie.

"Rose told me she is an angel from Heaven. I told her that I love angels!" Jace added, "Do you think she knows Daddy?"

"Maybe you should ask her next time," Marie said with a sad smile.

+++

Two days later Marie's cousin, Paula, came by with the bucket full of cleaning supplies, rags and five rolls of paper towels and said, "Cuz, put me to work?"

Marie was so delighted to see Paula again. They bear-hugged each other with a long embrace. They were about the same age and went through kindergarten, grade school, and high school together. They were thick as thieves. Paula released Marie, stepped back and with a big infectious smile on her face said, "Love ya cuz!"

After Paula and Marie removed the protective plastic sheet on the large countertop, they gave it a good washing. Marie said to Paula, "Listen...can you hear Jacelyn talking to herself?"

Paula nodded.

"She does it almost every time we're here," said Marie. "It's her invisible friend, Rose."

Paula looked at Marie and laughed. "Oh...OK...who had the Barbie doll and played dress-up and make-believe?" They both cracked up and Marie gave her a light noogie on the arm. They laughed even harder.

It was a fun afternoon full of hard work, laughs, some tears from wonderful memories, and Jace running back and forth. Between her little jobs she had and the milk and cookies on the table, Jace would then run off to the bathroom and the storage area where she liked to play.

"She's talking up a storm again, PB," as Marie liked to call her cousin, shaking her head from side-to-side with a smirk.

"At least she has an invisible friend to keep her company while we get a lot of work done," Paula chuckled, throwing a *sugine* (slang for kitchen towel) at Marie's head. They both laughed, but they got so much accomplished.

When they began to wind down for the day, Marie called Jacelyn, "Come-on, hunny, we gotta get ready to go home and have dinner. Noni made your favorite rice with Bolognese sauce and freshly grated parmesan."

"Yum, that sounds good Mommy...can Rose come with us?"

"Sure, go and ask her if she wants to join us," said Marie with a warm smile.

A short time later Jace came back out front to the café with a sad look on her face.

"What's wrong Jace?"

"Rose must have gone home, she's not back there," a disappointed Jace sighed.

"That's OK, hunny. You can invite her next time."

+ + +

A few days later, Marie was heading back to the café, after picking up Jacelyn at Mrs. Carey's Kindergarten class on Samoset Street.

"How was your day, Jace?"

"It was fun Mommy!" she blurted out, with an ear-to-ear smile. "We made postcards to give to people we love...so they know we love them."

"Aww, how special is that?" Marie grinned. "Can I see them?"

Jacelyn spread the handmade, hand cut, construction paper postcards out on the counter with the name of each person she was giving it to.

"Those are so adorable, my little angel." Marie blushed with pride. "Tell me all about those people you're giving them to."

Jacelyn never missed her cue to jump right in and take charge. "Well Mommy, of course this one with the red cardinal and Jesus' cross, is for Daddy. Do you think he will like it?"

"I think he'll love it, hunny." All Marie could do was shake her head and bite her lower lip to think at five years old, *This little child is an old soul.*

Jacelyn proceeded to lay out the other cards, her tongue sticking out at the corner of her mouth as she counted. "This one's for you Mommy, then one for No-ni." Jacelyn continued to show her cards for Grammy and Nana and some of her cousins.

The last postcard she held up was that of an elderly woman leaning on a counter with grey hair, not fragile by any means. She drew her as being very stoic and strong.

When Marie got to this postcard, she looked at it, tilted it from side-to-side to see if she could make out who the woman on the card was. After a few minutes, Marie looked at Jace and said, "Sweetie, who is this lady?"

Jace knew her mommy would ask. "That's Rose, my friend. I think she will like this card."

"Does she visit you often, hunny?" Marie inquired.

"Just when we are here at the café...sometimes we talk, other times she just sits and smiles at me.

Why, Mommy, did I do something wrong?" Jace said in a soft pitched voice.

Marie knew she needed to change gears and drive around this conversation with her five-year-old.

"No, hunny, you did nothing wrong. You're my and Daddy's angel. Let's get to work!"

+++

About five days before the unofficial opening, Marie, Noni, and Jacelyn were back at the café sweeping, washing the floors, and of course, Noni was dusting. The two ladies were working away, and Jacelyn was just keeping herself occupied.

Jacelyn walked over to the dessert case, as if being guided. She bent down and with her little hand she scraped with her fingernails at the edge of an envelope slightly sticking out from the bottom. She pulled the yellow envelope out, picked it up, and walked it over to her mother.

"What's this Jace?"

"It's an envelope I found under the desserts," she said pointing in the direction of the dessert case. "Rose told me to get it and give it to you."

"Are you and Rose still talking my little angel?"

"Yes Mommy, she is so excited that you are opening my café soon."

"Your café?" Marie chuckled.

"Well, it has my name on it!" Jacelyn said with a big smile, showing all her tiny teeth and squinting her eyes.

Marie chuckled, "Oh, so are you going to pay the bills, my little one?"

"Well, um, no, that's what mommies are for."

Marie stood there with a baffled look on her face. Upon opening the envelope, she looked inside and there was an old photograph. Pulling it out she saw a young couple, no older than teenagers. The boy and girl, with big smiles, appeared to be in what looked like a European café.

As she held it up, she noticed in the background behind the café bar was an espresso machine. She looked from the photo to the antique espresso machine at her café and back again a couple times.

She called Noni over from her ritual dusting. "Ida, look at this photo Jace found. Do you know who these two people are? The young woman looks familiar."

Noni took the photo and looked at it. Her eyes started to tear up. "Oh my, this is my Aunt Generosa and that must be Caesar. Oh my goodness! Where did you find it Jacelyn?"

"I found it under there," she said pointing again to the dessert case.

"And Rose told you it was there?"

"Yes, Mommy."

Andrew Louis Botieri

Marie was astounded! "Now look at the espresso machine in the back of the bar...that's the same one sitting right here," she said enthusiastically. "It must have been in the crate that Luca shipped from Italy. It could have easily fallen out and slid underneath the case when it was being unloaded."

They kept staring at it in amazement with smiles on their faces. Then Marie said, "It must have gotten a little wet or something because there's a strange blue haze around Generosa and Caesar in the photo. This is amazing!" Marie reached over and grabbed an empty picture frame, inserted the photograph of her great-aunt and Caesar and proudly placed it in front of the antique espresso machine next to the index card.

+ + +

That night after dinner, Marie and Noni continued to talk about the photo Jacelyn had found. "That is so incredible, I still can't believe it!" Marie said.

As she finished her sentence, Noni said, "I'll be right back." She got up from the kitchen table and went into her bedroom. She came back out minutes later with her family picture book. "This photo was taken of Generosa at age seventy-five in Renazzo."

"She is so beautiful," gushed Marie.

Noni continued showing Marie some other pictures of different family members from Italy. Marie put the picture of Generosa to the side, on the table. As she looked at picture after picture, she was just so proud. She had family in another country. Her heart panged; she missed her Anthony right now more than ever. *I wish Anthony and I could have visited my family over there,* she thought to herself.

At that moment, Jace padded into the kitchen to ask for something sweet to eat before bed. As she walked up to the kitchen table, she looked at the picture of Generosa and pointed at it and said with excitement, "Mommy, Mommy, that's my friend Rose!" Marie and Noni looked at each other in stunned amazement.

"Jace, you mean your invisible friend Rose from the café?" Marie nervously inquired.

"Yes, Mommy, she's such a nice lady...she's my angel!"

Noni grinned and with a tear in her eye said, "I told you; your little Jacelyn is truly a connection to the past. I could just feel it."

"Are you sure Jace?" Marie asked.

"Yes Mommy, I'm sure!"

24

Strange Lights Appear

At twenty-five years of age, Officer Mike Almeida had recently graduated from the police academy and was excited to get hired by the Plymouth Police Department; the town he grew up in. Mike was about six foot two, a solid 195 pounds, black curly hair, light brown eyes, and a mischievous smile. He was very athletic in high school where he played both football and baseball.

A few years earlier, he married his high school sweetheart, Cheryl. They had just bought a little house in North Plymouth, and he couldn't wait to start his new job. His wife commented on how handsome he looked in his "blues." Mike loved his town and all the people in it.

Mike's beat would be patrolling the downtown Plymouth area on foot and by cruiser from 3:00 p.m. to 12:00 midnight. He was so excited, not just to start the new job, but he had known most of the shop owners since he was a kid and looked forward to popping his head in to say hi to them.

Mike was the younger cousin of Marie on her dad's side. He was very close to Coach Tony, as he and so many of his friends called their baseball coach. He had attended the funeral service with his family, like most people in Plymouth.

On this day, he walked down South Russell Street on his way to Court Street after parking his patrol car, then a right toward Main Street. He crossed the road and stopped by to surprise his cousin who was opening up her new café.

As he opened the door and walked in, the bell above the door chimed. He looked over and saw Marie behind the counter.

"Congratulations for getting a job on our police force!" She looked up and beamed smiling like a kid. She came racing out from behind the counter, as she brushed off her apron covered in flour and gave him a big hug.

"So how are you making out, Marie?"

"I'm doing OK, Mike...I have my good days and bad days, but now that I've decided to open my café, it'll keep me busy bringing smiles to those who come in."

"You always were one to take care of others before yourself," he said. "The downtown will be my beat, so I will be able to keep an eye on things for you.

"I see you named the café after Jacelyn...that's very cool."

Marie smiled and said, "I was looking for a name that connected me to Anthony, and I couldn't think of a better one." As she said this, her eyes started to tear up.

Mike reached over and gave her a big hug and said, "All Tony ever talked about was you, Jacelyn, and the Red Sox, of course." He laughed and added, "So I know he'll be smiling down on the two of you...watching your success."

"Wait a minute," Marie said as she went behind the counter to grab him a cup of coffee in a to-go cup.

"Thanks for the coffee, how much?" He hoisted the cup in the air.

"I can't charge you; we're related!" Marie said with a chuckle. "Plus, I'm not legally open yet!" They both laughed.

"Well, I gotta get to work...but thanks for the coffee. I look forward to seeing you on my rounds Marie."

As Mike was walking out the door, he called over his shoulder, "Next time I'm buying."

+ + +

A couple days after Mike first stopped by the café, he was making his rounds at about 11:00 p.m. All the businesses along Court and Main Streets were closed and only a few night lights could be seen gleaning out of their store fronts. It was a cool September night, with a nice ocean breeze coming up North Street from the harbor, it felt refreshing. But it also brought in a little fog with it.

He loved the fact he could walk around historic Plymouth and keep a watch on things. Knowing his Pilgrim history, he knew that Myles Standish and his men patrolled the gated plantation and fort not far from where he stood on Court Street.

As he turned south on Court from Brewster Street, he could see the 1820 courthouse lit up in the background and the row of businesses to his left. As he crossed Court on the west side of the street, he crossed over South Russell Street, and as he stepped up on the curb, he noticed a faint blue light coming from Jace's Café's front window. The café had not yet opened so he thought Marie must've left a light on.

As he came closer to the window, the light disappeared. *That's strange,* he said to himself. When he got to the café, he shined his flashlight inside the picture window and looked around. Next, he reached over to check the door. It was locked. "Hmmm...Maybe a light burned out?" he mumbled.

He even walked around the back to make sure the door was secure as well. Officer Mike took out his small pocket notepad and jotted the occurrence down to let Marie know the next day when he stopped by.

The following day around 4:00 p.m., Mike walked into Jace's Café during his beat to say hi to Marie and to ask about the blue light he saw the night before.

"I saw the strangest thing last night," as he retold the story. "Do you have a blue light somewhere in here?" he said, waving his outstretched arm across the café.

"I don't think so," Marie said inquisitively. "Why?"

"Hmmm…that's real strange," he said, scratching his head. "It was as if it knew I was there and then just shut off. Can I walk around?"

"Sure."

Mike went from the front of the café to the back, looking at lights, around the corners. He then looked at Marie, "So you have no blue lights in any of your appliances?"

"Not that I know of Mike."

"OK, guess I'll keep an eye on things. If I see it again, I'll let you know."

As he got ready to leave Marie offered him a piece of her homemade blueberry buckle, she had just taken out of the oven.

He received it with a grateful smile, took a bite and said, "Wow, this is better than my mother's, but don't tell her that." They both chuckled.

+ + +

Over the next couple days, not only had Officer Mike seen the strange light emanating from the café's front window, but now other people who were driving by late at night noticed the light too. Some even called into the Police Station. Others were popping into Marie's café to say they saw a strange blue light coming from her store front window. The phenomenon was becoming the talk of the town.

It seemed the blue light always emanated from the front of the café, usually late at night, well after closing. Marie would walk around her café trying to figure out the mystery light, but to no avail.

+ + +

One night around 11:30 p.m. while on the last leg of his beat, Mike walked up Chilton Street and started heading south on Court toward Shirley Square. He looked south and saw the mysterious blue light once again emanating from Jace's Café. As he drew closer, he thought he saw a dark shadow, or shadows emerging from the café and start walking south.

Mike's walk turned into a jog and then a run as he tried to catch up to the mysterious figures. As Mike got to North Street, the figures turned right about fifty yards in front of him, into Town Square, right after M&M's Sporting Goods.

He then broke into a full run, his flashlight leading the way, and when he turned the corner, he saw nothing. He kept running until he hit the steps to Burial Hill, just to the right of the historic stone Mayflower Meetinghouse Church where the Pilgrim's first built their wooden Meetinghouse back in 1621. Three steps at a time he bounded up the stone stairs. All the while his flashlight sweeping left then right across the many ancient headstones. Again, nothing.

Mike called out, "I saw you and I will find you!" He sat on the hill bewildered. *What is going on?* Then he started doubting himself...*Did I see what I thought I saw?* The shadows just disappeared. He took off his police hat, scratched his head and thought, *Man I need a vacation.* Mike made a note in his police log, leaving out the "man I need a vacation" part.

+ + +

The next day, before Mike went on duty, he stopped by Jace's Café to speak with Marie. When he opened the door, the bell chimed, and Marie looked up from cleaning her pastry case. She greeted him with her usual bright smile. Mike returned a subdued grin.

"What's wrong?" She said.

Mike took off his police hat, shrugged his shoulders and said, "I'm not sure Marie, it's going to sound crazy."

"What will?" Marie said tentatively.

"Well, last night about 11:45, after I finished my last walk around before my shift ended, I was coming up Brewster Street, and as I turned south on Court, I saw not only that blue light coming from your café, but I saw...I think I saw, two people or shadows either coming out of your café or at least stepping out from inside the doorway. So, I followed them."

Mike told Marie his story, and she just sat there dumbfounded. Mike then went over to her door to see if it might have been tampered with. It showed no signs of forced entry.

"I just can't make hide nor hair of this Marie; it just doesn't make any sense."

+ + +

The next night was a full moon, a blood moon some would call it. Officer Mike was doing his rounds; he could see most of downtown, all lit up from the moon with a light, misty fog floating over the area, maneuvering in and around the store fronts. It was nights like this that he preferred, as the moon lit up his whole surroundings. Though tonight's moon had a hazy, fuzzy appearance due to the fog, creating a still, eerie feel to the downtown.

As he approached the café, he saw the blue glowing light emanating from her store front again. The light spewed out the front picture window as well as the side windows on North Street. It seemed more intense, brighter than before. As he approached, he could see a couple of shadows dancing off the blue light inside. He immediately called into dispatch to report what he was seeing. Dispatch asked if he wanted them to send a patrol car around. He hesitated. For some reason he felt no adrenaline rush of panic or fear. He felt a sense of calm come over him, as if someone had wrapped him in a warm blanket. He told them to hold off until he investigated a little further.

He went to the nearby payphone and called Marie. The phone rang and rang. Eventually Marie answered the phone on her nightstand and in a groggy voice said, "Hello?"

"Marie it's Mike Almeida...can you get down to your shop, like right now?"

Marie was panicked. "Is it on fire?"

"No," he said. "I am not sure why I'm calling you, but I think I'm supposed to."

"Mike you're making no sense," Marie said loudly into the phone.

"I can't explain it Marie. A voice is telling me to call you and get you down here. I think I saw those two figures, this time inside your café."

Marie looked over at the clock, it registered midnight. "You're the cop, you're supposed to handle this," she scolded him.

"I know it sounds crazy, but something is telling me you belong here tonight, to see this, to witness this."

Marie said, "I'll be there in ten minutes."

She hung up the phone, jumped out of bed, got dressed, then woke Noni and told her what was going on. Noni had the same look on her face as she did the day when Jacelyn was introduced to the whole family after being born. And in Marie's head she could hear her Ida say, *She will be a connection to the past.*

Marie cocked her head inquisitively and her Ida just smiled. At that moment, the panic Marie had felt from Mike's phone call disappeared. She looked at Noni and just said, "I love you my little Ida," Marie bolted down the stairs and out the front door.

Marie pulled up to a parking space a couple of stores down from her café, where she saw Mike pacing back and forth. Mike pointed over to Shirley Square, where what seemed like an elderly couple, walking near her café arm in arm, as if taking a midnight stroll.

Marie looked at Mike, and said, "Well?"

"I think they came out of your café," Mike said, "I know it sounds crazy, but by the time I ran up here from Brewster Street, they appeared to walk out of your café, and there they are."

"They look like a little old couple just out for a walk, Mike," Marie said exhaustedly.

"Ya at midnight?" Mike said, "but look closer, they have that same blue light around them that I always see coming from your café. Can you see it? Like, I said Marie, it's really weird."

Marie looked over and saw the blue light engulfing the elderly couple. Mike and Marie crossed Court Street to the front of her café. Mike put his flashlight up to the picture window to illuminate the inside just to make sure. The copper espresso machine gleamed back at them, a blue light engulfing it.

They continued to follow the mysterious couple past Shirley Square and across Middle Street, past the Colonial Restaurant, following at a safe distance. The mysterious couple were still walking arm in arm. At one point the old woman, with her white hair and scarf, glanced back at Mike and Marie.

Marie stopped dead in her tracks.

"What is it?" Mike whispered.

"I'm not 100 percent sure Mike, but she looks familiar."

"What do you mean she looks familiar; do you know her?"

"She just looks and feels familiar." Marie's head started to spin, and she felt a little lightheaded.

"Are you alright?" Mike said with concern, as he reached for her right shoulder to help keep her steady.

"Ya...I'm OK," she said with a hint of bewilderment as she drew out the I'm OK. "I...I...just have this funny feeling that something important is going to happen tonight...like this is all supposed to be occurring...as if it's meant to be, just like you said Mike."

Marie wasn't sure what to think. Hearing Noni in her head, *Jacelyn is a connection to the past*, and Anthony saying, *follow your heart, it's the best compass of all.*

As they continued to follow the couple, they realized they were not a threat. As Marie got closer, she worked up the nerve and called out, "Aunty Generosa? Aunty Generosa?"

As they got closer, the elderly couple stopped and turned to face Mike and Marie. Mike and Marie stopped in their tracks at the corner of Leyden and Main Streets across the street from the post office building. Marie was stunned.

"Yes, it is me, my little Marie. You look so much like your grandmother. Is she doing well?" Generosa had no trouble speaking English.

At the same time, Marie was speechless. A rush of emotions hit her like a ton of bricks, as tears began streaming down her face, Marie said, "But, but how?...Why?..."

"It's very simple my dear...Caesar and I never stopped loving each other, even after he was killed during the war. I had asked to be buried next to him when I died so we could at least be side-by-side forever. I thought we would unite once I was buried next to him. But I wasn't sure, and as it turns out, it was only the magic of the espresso machine that finally brought us together.

"For some special reason and by the Grace of God, when we had our picture taken in front of that old espresso machine back in Renazzo so many decades ago, that picture that now sits in your café, something magical happened. Our spirits or souls were transferred into that machine from that photograph. Even at my café in Renazzo, people would tell me they would see a faint blue light coming from the café many hours after I closed. At first, I didn't know what to think.

"When I came across the old photograph of Caesar and me, I prayed and prayed for us to be united in some way. I guess God answered our prayers. That was Caesar trying to come through. I knew that if my nephew, Luca, didn't stay with the café, our hopes of reuniting would never happen. So, on my instructions after I passed away, I had my nephew send the espresso machine here to you, maybe your magic and the magic of Jacelyn could bring us together, once and forever."

Marie said, "So you are the older woman, that Jacelyn always talked about, that she would have conversations with back at the café...her imaginary friend, Rose? Generosa...Rose...I get it!"

"Yes, that was me...but I was not imaginary Marie. It was the innocent spirit of Jacelyn that allowed me to connect with her and through that allow Caesar and me to finally reunite."

Marie staggered back a few steps, Mike kept her from falling over. Mike added, "So the blue light I kept seeing all those nights was the two of you?"

Caesar now spoke up, "Yes, it took us many tries. We even know you chased after us," looking over at Officer Mike, "into the cemetery, but we weren't able to fully unite yet. Tonight, we were finally able to come through the magic of the espresso machine together. We needed our lovely Marie to be here for the final connection to be completed."

Marie couldn't stop crying, Generosa leaned over and hugged her great-niece. "Your Noni told you Jacelyn was a connection to the past...and she was right. God brought your little miracle baby into this world so that Caesar and I would someday reunite in everlasting love."

With that, Generosa kissed Marie on the forehead and said, "Mia Bella."

"But Aunty Generosa, I have so, so many questions, so many...."

"All in due time my dear. There will be other nights." Generosa placed her hand on Marie's arm.

Marie felt a surge of energy flow from Generosa through her body. She felt at peace.

At that moment Generosa and Caesar smiled at both Marie and Mike, locked arms, turned around, and walked about ten feet down Main Street, crossed over Leyden Street, disappeared into the fog, and vanished...forever in love and happiness.

Marie and Mike just stood there and looked at each other in utter amazement. "Did that just happen?" Marie stuttered.

Mike took off his police hat, scratched his head and said, "I'm not sure how to report this. I guess I don't."

+ + +

So next time you're in Downtown Plymouth and you see an old couple late at night with a blue aura around them, locked arm in arm walking down Court or Main Street, make sure you go over and say hi to Generosa and Caesar.

Epilogue (2001)

Jace's Café opened a few days after the encounter with Generosa and Caesar. It was a huge success and the café, especially on weekends, had a waiting line outside. Marie and Jacelyn continued with life in Plymouth and at the café. Jace was now ten years old and a handful. Marie could see so much of Anthony in her beautiful daughter and her mannerisms.

A few years later, Noni would pass away at the ripe old age of ninety-seven. A big piece of Marie's heart went with her. Marie would eventually take over Steven's Florist, next to her café and break the adjoining wall down to double the size of her café. She now employed ten people, which allowed her some days off.

On her days off she would stop by the local flower shop and grab some fresh white calla lilies, one of Noni's favorites. She and Jace would drive over to the cemetery, pull up to her headstone, and place the flowers in the front. A small smile came to her face, as all the memories of her "little Ida" came rushing at her. They would then stop by Anthony's gravesite and Jace would tell her daddy all that was going on in her life.

Marie never remarried, though she did meet a great guy who made her laugh so hard she would snort.

Marie's brother, Mickey, went on to be drafted by the Boston Red Sox farm team in Pawtucket, R.I. after many years of bouncing around to different teams in Triple A Baseball. Old for a rookie at thirty-two, in 2004 he was called up to the big leagues and got to pinch hit during the Red Sox World Series victory over the St. Louis Cardinals. The Red Sox broke the "Curse of the Bambino" referring to the curse that followed the Red Sox for eighty-six years, after their owner, Harry Frazee, sold Babe Ruth in 1919 to the New York Yankees in exchange for $125,000 in cash. In 1918, the Red Sox had just won the World Series. It was very controversial and led to much speculation of Frazee having money issues. Another curse that was broken, was Mickey fulfilled his grandfather, Nino and his father's quest to make it to "The Big Dance."

Marie would see Generosa and Caesar on occasion strolling down Main Street late at night, sometimes she would engage them, but most times she didn't interrupt them. She'd let them have their romantic walks in silence. All in all, life was good in Plymouth.

End Notes

[i] Ross King, The Shortest History of Italy; The Experiment, April 16, 2024

[ii] David Nicolle and Raffaele Ruggeri, The Italian Army of World War I, Osprey Publishing, March 25, 2003, page 3

[iii] David Nicolle and Raffaele Ruggeri, The Italian Army of World War I, Osprey Publishing, March 25, 2003, pages 3-4, 175-176, 180-181

[iv] David Nicolle and Raffaele Ruggeri, The Italian Army of World War I, Osprey Publishing, March 25, 2003, pages 3-4

[v] Ancos, Life in Italy, 1900-1940; (https://lifeinitaly.com/italy-1900/); Helga Dosa updated on March 6, 2021

[vi] C N Trueman, Italy In 1900 (https://www.historylearningsite.co.uk/modern-world-history-1918-to-1980/italy-1900-to-1939/italy-in-1900/) 25 May 2015. 6 Feb 2021

[vii] Chewy Editorial, 8 Italian Dog Breeds, Updated: January 26, 2022. Gatto's breed is a Spinone Italiano. Also known as the Italian Pointer. A very sociable dog with a docile temperament. The Spinone loves to be around family and activity. He is a relatively low maintenance dog.

[viii] David Nicole, The Italian Army of War World I, Osprey Publishing, March 25, 2003, page 3

[ix] Ibid. pages 3-4

[x] Military History of Italy During World War I (https://en.wikipedia.org/wiki/Military_history_of_Italy_during_World_War_I#:~:text=Almost%20a%20year%20after%20the,the%20terrain%20favoured%20the%20defender)

[xi] Plymouth Cordage Company (https://www.plymouthcordageco.org/#:~:text=The%20Plymouth%20Cordage%20Company%2C%20a,by%20the%20late%2019th%20century)

Other than the specific endnotes attributed to research in this book, all other facts were culled from a variety of sources in Wikipedia.

Acknowledgments

There are so many people I would like to acknowledge in shaping the final words you have just read in my first novel. First, I need to thank and Praise God and His Son Jesus, my Christ, for saving my life on June 29, 2000 and giving me a second chance at life. From that experience, came my first book *A Celebration of Life: A Story of Hope, a Miracle & The Power of Attitude*. A wonderful Blessing!

Second, my mom and dad, Betty and Don Botieri, for their constant belief in me, their love and guidance bestowed upon me while on earth and their continued hand from Heaven above. My Guardian Angel, Andrew Balboni, who watches down on me. My grandparents, Nino and Ida Botieri, who continue to be my heroes and inspiration. The "Aunties"...need I say more? My wonderful siblings, Carol, Karen (Marie), and Michael (Mickey), who in my time of need have always been there by my side. And all my family: my cousin Larry Richardson, a writer and screen writer in his own right, who read my manuscript in its early stages and shared his valued advice. Thanks Cuz! Lee Hartman, Planning Director at Plymouth Town Hall, for helping me with old photos of downtown Plymouth and the waterfront as I crafted my story.

To my famiglia in Cento and Renazzo, Italy for being an inspiration and a part of my story. Also, a big shoutout to my editor, consultant and faithful friend

Claudia Gere, who helped me self-publish my first book and when we met to discuss the writing of *The Magical Espresso Machine*, she just paused and said, "WOW!" Thank you Claudia for your patience as we traveled this journey together.

And last but not least, to my great-grandparents Generosa (Trocchi) and Caesar Bottieri, who without them emigrating to the historic waterfront town of Plymouth, Massachusetts in the 1890s, this novel would never have happened. When I first met this side of my famiglia in Renazzo, Italy in 2016, they introduced me to two other ways the name Botieri is spelled— Bottieri and Buttieri. It took discovering my great-parents' marriage certificate to see Caesar's last name was spelled Bottieri. For this story, however, I elected to use Buttieri. Love to all! (Amore a tutti!)

+ + +

Please visit my website: www.andrewbotieri.com to purchase either one of my books. Each copy is autographed and personalized. Or visit Amazon for a Kindle version. To contact me directly via email: Andrew@AndrewBotieri.com

Ciao!!

www.ingramcontent.com/pod-product-compliance
Lightning Source LLC
Chambersburg PA
CBHW051822020726
47502CB00005B/1590